The Insolent Boy

The Insolent Boy

John Stiles

INSOMNIAC PRESS

Edited by Richard Almonte
Copy edited by Lorissa Sengara
Designed by Mike O'Connor
Book cover by Marcus Robinson
Author photo and rabbit photo by Paul Perrier

National Library of Canada Cataloguing in Publication Data

Stiles, John
The insolent boy

ISBN 1-894663-01-2

I. Title.

PS8587.T554I57 2001 C813'.6 C2001-930396-3
PR9199.3.S7975I57 2001

The publisher gratefully acknowledges the support of the Canada Council, the Ontario Arts Council and Department of Canadian Heritage through the Book Publishing Industry Development Program.

Printed and bound in Canada

Insomniac Press, 192 Spadina Avenue, Suite 403,
Toronto, Ontario, Canada, M5T 2C2
www.insomniacpress.com

This novel is dedicated to Joan Florey
in memory of P.H. Walker and O.A. Stiles

This book could not have been finished without the love and support of my parents David and Wicky, Buds and Susie. I am forever thankful for the guidance and support of Corb, Dug, T.J. and Mike, Jennifer Barclay, Bruce Moffit, Marcus Robinson, The Gladstone Hotel '97, The Imperial Library Pub '00, Veridiana Toledo, Flavia, a rabbit named D2, Mike O'Connor and Richard Almonte.

CHAPTER 1

"No." I turned and glared at the rector.

"Are you sure, Selwyn?"

I pouted and nodded at Bee, who fussed with me. She stooped and had another go at me with her hankie.

"The other children may be mean to you, dearie. Why don't you wait till next year?"

I pushed her away and stood on tiptoes. I braced myself against the back of the chesterfield and stared out the sitting-room window at a brigade of three-year-old boys wrapped tight in blue woollen tunics. They hopped about like pigeons.

"We thought it best to wait a year," said Bee, smoothing my hair over.

"No," I said again, dropping the Bible story to the floor and staring back out the window. "I want to go to nursery school now."

Bee eyed the old rector. "We'll discuss it after tea, dear."

Bee stood in the larder and poured her husband a glass of sherry. "Selwyn is too sensitive to be with other children," she said.

The old rector sipped and cradled his drink. "We don't want to spoil him, Gwendolyn. If we isolate him from other children we may spoil him."

"But he's so awkward, Hugh. And he has a temper. The other children may be little brutes to him."

"Or he them," the rector replied, puffing on his pipe.

Chapter 2
The Christmas Pageant

Since I was only three years old and had been largely confined to the grounds of the old rectory I had no clue of how to behave or what to say to the rest of the children who stood stiff and stared at me as I came in through the clogged doorway of the Penny Creek Nursery School. So I remained at salute, packed tight into a mauve snowsuit, and fixed my eyes on the mass of three- and four-year-old blank faces before me. The teacher, Miss Tillotson, eyed me uncomfortably, while a handsome dark-haired boy trotted neatly past me and placed a single molasses cookie on the lip of the teacher's desk.

"Thank you Luke," said the teacher, smiling pleasantly at the child, who beamed back at her like a thrown toy. Since I was hot and miserable in that snowsuit and uncertain of why I hadn't been welcomed into the class or doted upon in the same way as that handsome child, I huffed loudly and unzipped myself, dropped my hat and mittens to the floor and hurried through the clogged coat rack towards Miss Tillotson's desk to help myself to that welcoming snack.

But as I wandered up to her Miss Tillotson stooped and whispered to me that the molasses cookie was not my cookie; it would be given out at the end of day to reward the day's best-behaved child. I was dismayed and embarrassed that the whole class had stood there and witnessed my gaffe. So I shrank where I stood and shuffled to the back of the class and sat with a group of glum two-year-olds who stared at me like I was a ghost. I told them to stop staring at me.

"Who are you?" they asked.

"Selwyn," I answered defiantly.

"Well, it's fall not winter," one of the kids chimed. "Why were you dressed up like a snowman?"

"Bee dressed me," I answered.

"Who is Bee?"

"My mummy," I replied. The little boys put their hands

over their mouths, kicked in their chairs and tittered like schoolgirls.

I sat there for the whole time, head down and sulking. I wrapped my feet around the legs of the chairs and pushed and kicked. Still not a word of acknowledgement from any of my classmates. Very soon I began to yawn loudly and fidget with the tablecloth and make little dunce's cones with the paper in fits of boredom. But still nothing, not even a simple smile from any of the other children. I sat indignantly in silence while a few of those little monkeys drew Halloween pumpkins and witches on the blackboard before me. Finally the handsome one, Luke, turned to me with a fierce glare. He passed me some white chalk.

"What's this for?"

"To draw a snowman with a snowsuit, silly."

I looked at him, eyes like slits. "Leave me alone," I bellowed loud as a foghorn.

When the end-of-day bell rang, I marched up to the front and stood at the teacher's desk with my hand outstretched, expecting that since I had endured this cruel lot, the prize cookie was mine. Again the teacher eyed me warily.

"Come forwards please, Luke," said Miss Tillotson.

I stood there in stunned silence while Luke Caldwell smugly marched past me and took his prize cookie back.

When I returned to the old rectory that night I sat at the table in the scullery and sulked. Bee stood over me, spooning custard into my bowl of plums.

"What is it dear?"

She bent down. I whispered in her ear.

"Oh," she responded, "you won't wear the snowsuit tomorrow, dearie."

"No," I droned, glumly. Then I whispered again.

"Ah," Bee smiled, "teacher and child were flirting, dear."

"Flirting?"

She paused. Seemed unsure. "Flirting can be done when you give gifts." She cackled a bit. "Why don't you take Miss Tillotson an apple? The September harvest has been marvellous this year and she might like an apple."

"Why?" I frowned.

"That's what children in nursery schools give their teachers to impress them."

Then Bee held my hand. Took me towards the cold room. She steadied herself and pointed. There in the cold dank room were bags and sacks of fruit and vegetables.

"You'll have to look carefully, dearie," she called, while I peered over the lip of the barrels and ransacked the burlap bags of harvest fruit. But there was not one good apple. Just crab apples, pears and a few plums.

The next day I marched into the nursery school with a satchel full of plums and crab apples and pears and arranged them all in a neat line at the end of Miss Tillotson's desk.

"Thank you..." said Miss Tillotson, a scarecrow in her long woollen skirt.

"Selwyn," I corrected, mortified that she had forgotten my name.

The classroom murmuring stopped and for a brief uplifting moment, faces raised. But when those little miseries saw it was just me their chins dropped to their chests and they set about scratching away in their colouring books again. I was humiliated, shattered by the utter dismal truth that I hadn't made the slightest positive impression on any of the cheery kids in the class.

By week's end I was miserable, shuffling in through the scullery and staring grimly into the cold rectory room at the burlap sacks of fruit and carrots and vegetables that were there.

"What is it Selwyn?" said Bee.

But I said not one word as I once again dropped vegetables and fruit into my little rucksack to take back to the nursery school.

Each and every morning during the late autumn I made a determined and grand entrance into the classroom. I sailed up to the teacher's wooden desk and deposited a single polished Gravenstein, a pair of husky Russets, a bland but oversized Spye, a small parcel of Bartlett pears, a fat green gourd and a trio of cucumbers, and arranged them all carefully in a little attractive pile. But instead of being nibbled at and passed around as samplers and treats, the fruit just sat. After a week the small pile became a mound. But still not a hint of attention from any of those kids.

"Left over from Thanksgiving?" remarked one parent, sweeping his child into his arms at the end of one school day.

"Would you like one?" replied Miss Tillotson, standing tensely beside the man.

But still not one word to me. Just other children who hid behind their mothers' skirts and glared at me.

Finally, after one grim afternoon of glum faces and a late autumn heat wave, we heard a loud drubbing at the window. There was a deafening shriek as Miss Tillotson ducked down while a marauding black army of fruit flies and angry wasps swarmed in through a crack in the window. While the teacher batted about her head in fright, Luke Caldwell watched in horror as a giant solitary wasp shuttled, like a space capsule, over that impressive mountain of untouched fruit and darted straight into his lunch bag. It buzzed violently, and then made an angry assault for Luke's handsome head of hair.

Hordes of hooded green drones followed the lead wasp like a cloud, and Luke went white as a sheet, then bolted out the classroom door past the ornaments on the lawn and crashed into the great stalks of cow corn outside. When the nursery-school superintendent arrived in a big blue sedan to help search for Luke in the great acreage of cow corn, he took one look at Miss Tillotson's honking red nose and began comforting Luke's mother, who was flailing her hands about her sides, blind with hysteria.

"Who is responsible for this?" he asked.

All heads turned towards me where I sat on the lawn, stuffing my face with plums.

"The rectory child," sniffed Miss Tillotson, holding her nose. The crowd of them turned, awaiting my reply. But instead of answering, I stood up straight and threw my hand out like a point. There in front of me was Luke Caldwell, sitting like a pylon in the back of the rectory car, bawling his eyes out. Seeing him in such a state of anxiety I immediately warmed to him and shot across the turf to greet him.

But when Luke saw me, standing there with my plums in my hands, he stepped out of the car, squeezed his mother's hand and went off again like a siren.

Soon I was so alienated and frustrated in that class that I secretly pinched the little sulker to try and get his attention. But instead of challenging me as I hoped he would, Luke pouted so monstrously that he soon had a crowd of fawning adults hovering over him. Seeing all those large burly women brushing and picking at the child I began to titter nervously behind them. But not one parent saw even a smidge of the humour in it. Finally Luke's mother could bear me no more. She turned on me.

"What have you done?" she bellowed.

I was outraged. I wanted to beetle across the room and climb onto the colouring table and tell them all that my mother, Bee, had told me a clever tale about a village orphan who had ridiculed the ruling emperor and instead of being punished, had been appointed to the wise emperor's court as a reward for his strength of character. But the parents who crowded around Luke would have none of it. I was told to go at once and sit at my own table near the back, where I sulked and made grim faces as the other children circled me to get to the loo.

I tried to hide my shame by feigning disinterest, but I could not contain myself in that seat. Finally I marched across the room and stencilled the name "Pip" on Luke's arm while we all waited to assemble for the preschool Christmas pageant.

"Owwww," Luke whined, dressed as Balthazar, one of the three wise men, in a flowing garish gown.

"Don't be such a baby," I hissed. "I was only trying to be your friend."

"Who told you to do that?" he said, shuffling towards me in his constricting satins.

Seeing his mother about to swoop in on me like a giant bat, I panicked. "That child there," I answered, pointing at a pack mule cowering beneath a giant Eaton's refrigerator box in the corner. While the two tots—wise man and Saviour—stood pouting at one another, I, dressed as the Star of Bethlehem, held my crown and teetered onto the stage. Miss Tillotson huddled near the curtains, whispering

> Star of wonder, Star of light
> Star of royal beauty bright...

I stood there. Stared at the lights. The entire community before me.

"I see the future..." I began to shake. "...and Father Christmas has plummeted into the sea." A sea of faces. Mouths opened. And babies began to cry.

Chapter 3

Despite concerns within the quiet community that the village rector and his wife were bringing up an unstable child, Hugh Davis and his wife Gwendolyn took great pains to call a meeting at the local village hall and convince the town's parents that my behaviour was neither obstinate nor disdainful, but rather evidence of a strong theatrical and musical leaning.

Instead of being punished me for my obstinence, I was encouraged to listen to the rousing strains of Mahler, Chopin, Liszt and various Italian operettas, which the rector played on an antique record player in my bedroom above the porch.

At first I was receptive to the encouragement and sang lustily along to the music. The Rector was so taken with my aptitude and clear singing voice that he delighted in telling his congregation of old ladies and farmers' families that his awkward son had sterling singing talent and had memorized whole passages of Madama Butterfly and Chopin's Military Polonaise.

But his continual praise of me during the latter part of the Anglican church service was eventually met with muted interest, grim stares and hushed whisperings.

Finally one old man from the back bellowed: "Show the child the cane!"

A few parishioners turned. The old man shrank in his seat. But the evidence against me was strong.

"The child needs guidance," said the packs of men talking on the steps of the village town hall.

"He needs friends," said Miss Tillotson to the Rector's wife after church.

Since I was deemed awkward and unmanageable amongst the other children, the rector and his wife decided that a child of my churlish nature would benefit from the wise and calming influence of seniors, and so I was soon paired with Miss Jess, the organist of St. Peter's Anglican Church. At first I was delighted with the idea. I thought Miss Jess would be the kindly old soul whom I remembered sitting high up near the altar in the church during my toddler years. But when the rector and Miss Jess came in through the mud room together I sensed a certain conviction in the old woman's stride. The kindly soul I had watched sitting behind the church organ settled into the seat beside me like a broody hen. She breathed heavily and pulled at her sausage fingers.

"Scales first, please," commanded Miss Jess. And so we went, like chicken and wood tit, singing and banging out the scales.

When the lesson finished, I threw my music in my satchel and bolted up the stairs. I sat at the top with my hands over my nose and mouth and tried to hold my breath until the church organist left. For two whole hours I sat at the top of the stairs. I wiped at the frost in the window and peered out at the laneway, counting silly games in my head and waiting for the rector to drive the old bird home.

I sulked and went blue in the face and buzzed like a trapped fly and I was soon miserable and freezing up there. But I was determined not to show my face until the old cancer was gone. Very soon I began to doze on those cold stairs and I dreamed of a little singing canary, released from its captivity into the open air. When I heard a car start I awoke with a jump and sailed down the stairs, near-starved and excited to tuck into my nightly treat. But there at the head of the dinner table was the old bird settled into my seat. I glared at Miss Jess. Then at Bee. I stamped my foot. It had been a neighbour's car that I had heard and not Miss Jess's.

"Look what Mrs. Caldwell just brought round," said Bee, holding up a large loaf of bread. "A goodwill gesture from Luke."

"Young Selwyn does sing beautifully, doesn't he?" interrupted Miss Jess, putting down her dark-rimmed glasses on the table.

"He does," nodded Bee, retreating to the scullery with the bread.

"Do you remember that young Welsh choirboy that used to tour round America?" Miss Jess smiled, suspiciously. "The one with the lovely clear voice?"

"Colin Jones?" said the rector.

"Whatever became of him, Hugh?"

"Manhood," replied the old rector, banging his pipe out at the table. While the lot of them laughed at my expense, I turned beet red and tried to burrow my way under the table. The rector tugged gently at my arm.

"Would you mind singing the grace, please, Selwyn?"

But I was so annoyed I sat stiff-backed and murdered it:

Oh the Lard is good to me
and so I thank the Lard
for giving me
the things I need
the sun and the rain
and the apple seed
the Lard is good to me

After dinner I tried to sleep in my bedroom above the porch but I was kept awake by the faint whispers of the rector and his wife conspiring to do something productive with me. So I crept up from my bed, covered my shoulders with a quilt and tiptoed across the creaking wooden floor towards the heating grate to see if I could listen in.

"You musn't push him Hugh. He is only five."

"But he has perfect pitch, Gwendolyn."

"Many young boys have good ears and clear voices, Hugh."

"Not all boys with that sort of talent are encouraged at a young age, Gwendolyn."

Above them, I stepped awkwardly on the landing and there was a loud creak throughout the house.

"Are you asleep, Selwyn?" the rector's wife called, as I froze like a statue and felt faint from lack of breath. "Are you asleep, dear?"

And with that I put my lips to the grate and went:

ZZZZZZZZZZZZZZZZZZZZZZZZZZZZZZ

like one of those green hornets right into it.

"Naughty, isn't he?" murmured Miss Jess.

"A challenge," corrected Bee.

I soon began to obsess about how long I would be expected to sing with the church organist, who was a bully and who whispered mean things to me when she played. I was so mad with frustration that I ran out to the back garden the next time she came. I climbed the wooden trellis over the lilac bushes and leapt into the air to try and roost like a starling in the branches of the maple tree. But instead of climbing to the top, I tipped from the lower branches like a stone. The rector came straight for me, collected me in his wheelbarrow and marched me back to the house, where, after Bee scraped the twigs off my knees and washed the dirt from behind my ears, the church organist was waiting for me at the piano.

"Scales first, please," said the old rector.

"I've never seen such dirty fingernails," said Miss Jess as I lifted the piano case for her.

The rector stood at the piano and sucked on his pipe and rumbled in that deep English baritone, "I'm the one to blame, Mildred. My eyes aren't what they were, you know."

"Surely the child knows what a washing basin is, Hugh."

And so it went. I would sigh and then listen to that ham-handed banging and she would pick at me till I closed my eyes and said that she should quit playing the piano because she wasn't getting any better at it.

"You are a rude child," she said.

It was a grim and bitter winter. I sat and near froze in my room above the porch and dreaded the coming Monday and Wednesday lessons. But when spring came, the birds in the trees began to twitter and my spirits raised. The rector told me that Miss Jess was called back to Britain to be with her sickly sister and there were whisperings amongst the old women in the congregation that she might not be coming back to Nova Scotia because she didn't feel like she was appreciated for what she did in the parish.

"Miss Jess will be missed," said the old rector when he got the phone call in the larder.

"Missed?" muttered Bee.

"Who will we have to replace her?" called Hugh, puffing on his pipe.

"I'm sure there'll be another lonely old widow who will want to come round, Hugh," Bee replied. She looked at me. "Are you alright, Selwyn?"

My eyes drew to slits as I stared at a faded deck of playing cards on the side table and imagined Miss Jess locked away in a small cottage, playing solitaire and freezing with a scarf over her head.

Bee went into the larder. She came back, hands behind her back. She was fussing with one of my birthday gifts, a longish rectangular box, which she held high. I stood on tiptoes, stretched for the present.

"Say please, Selwyn."

"Pees."

"Dear oh dear." The two old bods stared at me as I ripped the box to bits. There on the hearth of the scullery was not the pellet gun I had pestered them for. Instead there was a scratched-up little violin.

The old rector had decided that since I could sing so well I should be presented with an instrument that required challenge. Despite my threat to make target practice of the thing, I stuck it under my chin and sawed away on it in frustration. Kind Mrs. Kessler became my violin instructor. Unlike with Miss Jess, I liked Mrs. Kessler a great deal because she was gentle with me and let me play with her two Siamese cats, who lay on the sofa in the sun and marched along her kitchen counters when I played. When the lesson was done Mrs.

Kessler sat me down at the table while she ironed her linens and treated me to a plate of her gingersnap cookies, which I hoarded in the lining of my little jacket when she wasn't looking. On the way home from the lesson I sat in the back of the rectory car munching on those cookies like a prince.

"Did Mrs. Kessler give you all those cookies, dear," said Bee, watching me in the rearview mirror.

I nodded, mouth full.

"I count seven cookies, Selwyn."

I stuffed another one in.

"I'm going to stop the car, dear, if you don't tell the truth."

I stuffed another one in.

"That's it!"

I stood at the side of the road while Bee frisked me. She then licked her hankie and had a go at my grubby face. I stamped my foot on the spot.

"I wish Mrs. Kessler was my mum and not you," I pouted, cheeks like a chipmunk.

"She can have you, young ruffian," said Bee, as she tried to join the front of my pants again.

But no matter how much I didn't want to go to those violin lessons, I hadn't the courage or the strength to disobey, and so I took solace in the the warm smell of Mrs. Kessler's apartment and the sweet smell of old ladies' perfume and those tasty cookies on which I munched and munched. As I put that thing under my chin and sawed along, my waistline surged like a balloon and the seams of my trousers split. My pant buttons burst and scattered across the floor while those two Siamese cats leapt from the counters and went after them. Still I held fast and sawed away. "Frère Jacques" graduated to "Claire de lune." "Claire de lune" became Vivaldi. Vivaldi graduated to Dvořák. I soon became so content and fat and good at the violin that Mrs. Kessler was serving tea in the sitting room and telling the rector and Bee that I would be much better placed in the high-school orchestra than studying with an old woman who hadn't taught the violin in years.

"It would be bad at his age to further alienate the child," said Mrs. Kessler to Bee after the lesson.

"You're going on a diet, Selwyn," said Bee, putting her hands on my rear end and squashing me back into the car.

And so because I had grown so plump Bee set me out into the back garden with the rector's wheelbarrow to weed and do chores around the rectory. I was miserable out there in the cold but Bee was strict, and I walked for miles round and round that back garden, picking up stones and twigs and seeds and garden twine and grimly throwing it all in the bin. Occasionally I would spot a child in a window staring at me and I would scowl in frustration and take the big overcoat I was wearing and pull the hood down over my head and drone like I was a madman lost in the woods. Each evening Bee would pull my jacket from my arms and hoist me onto an old grocers scale.

"I'm not sending you to that school plump, young man," she said as she went to the refrigerator and charted my progress on a church calendar. After a month I was down a stone. The rector lifted my shirt and fingered my ribs, which were sticking through my shirt.

"You don't want to take it too far, Gwendolyn," said the rector, puffing on his pipe.

"I think he'll fit in fine," said Bee, capping a tin of sweets which she hid from me.

As I sat in the back of the rectory car, staring out the window at the rows and rows of apple orchards and the white churches and Cape Blomidon jutting like a clay nose out into the sea, I held the violin case tight to my lap. I dreaded meeting the schoolchildren and I hoped that the rectory car would just keep merrily on its way up past the red farm silo and the blue dairy farm and circle its way home to my beloved and safe white wooden rectory. But when I got to the school the band teacher greeted me in a grand fashion and brought me into the band room and introduced me to the assembled masses. I stared straight at my toes.

"Look up and say hello to the children, Selwyn, dear," said Bee.

But I would not.

"He's a rare one, isn't he?" said the school principal, who stood stiffly with the teacher and the other students.

I felt uncomfortable the whole time I was in that band and soon I began staring at the windows of the school fantasizing about how I could climb the tuba case against the wall, stick my legs through the window, drop down into the school parking lot and bolt for the woods. As the weeks passed, I sat there becoming more and more frustrated and paranoid.

"Everybody quiet." Faces turned and stared at me while Mr. Cromwell, an expectant man, raised his hands and stabbed the air.

"Trill please." The tall grade nines snickered. A fluff of hair. Exasperation on a pink face. Tapping on the music stand.

"Do you see, class? Do you see?"

Kids grumbled. Horn blasts. A cornet spritzed and emptied. A fat girl blew into the tuba.

"No. No. No." Mr Cromwell came round pressing fingers over keys and bridges. "Selwyn, trill please," he said.

I threw my hand out like a glove. Steadied myself. The sound of mosquitoes. Millions of them.

"Beautiful, Selwyn."

But I was not happy there with those children who stared murder at me.

I couldn't win. I was so good at the violin that the old rector tried to audition me for the Nova Scotia Youth Orchestra. But I wouldn't have it; I stood on the porch, dressed in my Sunday finest, and I finally let the violin case drop from my hands.

"Selwyn, the viola," said the rector's wife, holding my coat in her hands.

"That's not a viola," I replied, "it's a violin."

"Well it's broken, dear."

"Good," I replied. And when she left to tell the rector of the accident, I jumped on the case and crushed the damned, useless thing.

As punishment for breaking the violin I was sent to my room, where I hid in the closet, hoping that they might think I had run away. But no police or child-welfare people appeared to rescue me and I soon found myself sitting in the dark closet all alone, scratching at the walls like a cat. Eventually I was summoned by the rector, who was reading through a hymn book in his study.

"What is it, Selwyn, that you dislike about the violin?"

"I hate the sound of it."

"Hate, Selwyn?"

"It depresses me, sir."

"Depresses you?" The old rector hummed a bit, then stopped. "Why is it that an instrument that moves and uplifts me depresses and frustrates you? Is there an instrument that doesn't depress you?"

"A pellet gun," I said.

"A pellet gun?"

The rector peered over his eyeglasses and sighed in a very gruff fashion. He put his book down, rolled up his sleeves. "Selwyn, do you see this scar?"

I walked towards him and he pulled back the sleeves of his work shirt and made me trace my fingers over the horrid purple thing on his forearm. I lowered my head.

"I do, sir."

"In the spring of 1942 I was sitting in a farmer's kitchen in rural France when I saw the underside of a German bomber move across the sky like a dark cloud," he said. "I ran like the clappers as soon as I saw it, to signal to my men who were resting in a nearby field. When I got to them I was too late;

the bomb had dropped from the sky and destroyed the barn where my best friend Gordie Gates had taken cover. Now I buried my best friend in a field of turnips and broken stone the next day, Selwyn." He looked at me, searching my face for signs that I understood the gravity of what he was saying. "Shrapnel is made of lead, the same lead that is shot from the chamber of a pellet gun. Would you mind telling me what it is that fuels this interest in guns?"

"I like the idea of something being forced out, sir."

"Forced out?" The rector nodded sagely. "Do you know how to blow a raspberry?"

"I do sir."

I blew one. Two. Three. I blew them all at him.

The next morning the old Rector marched me next door to the home of the retired schoolteacher, who repaired my violin strings in his basement. The old grump adjusted his glasses, took my face in his hands and squeezed my cheeks together.

"Reverend," he said in a gravelly voice, "the child has a good mouth."

I was court-martialed and sentenced to one year of standing at the top of the creaky rectory stairwell, blowing angry morning raspberries into Major Hugh Davis's brass military flugelhorn.

Chapter 4

From the time I had been in nursery school through my first few years at elementary school I made several unsuccessful attempts to befriend the village boys, who had branded me a pariah since the Christmas pageant. Since I desperately wanted friends, I turned my attention towards the girls, whom I admired when they came to church and sat in the pews with their hair in frilly ribbons, and who chirped sweetly up to their parents. But they always ignored me when I walked up to them with a list of questions or else they told the teacher I was pestering them. By the age of seven I was shattered by my continual dismissal by the other children. I was ready to leap off the iron girders of the Cornwallis Bridge and sink like an old fridge into the sludge and muck. Then one day, while I was plotting a dramatic leap from that bridge, I stumbled upon a dusty chest which contained the rector's old army gear: one tin cup, a pair of polished black boots, a sharp prodding implement and a pair of field glasses which I held up to the light and buffed. I sat in the rector's room for the bulk of the afternoon, fascinated by the bits and bobs that were in there. As I sat there I remembered the war stories the rector had told me the day he had given me his military flugelhorn. I imagined the dark skies and running men and shouts of fear and finally the peace that settled over the fields after the bombing. I imagined a brave and clever survivor lying in the grass with those field glasses scanning a safe country house with a lovely and kind nurse in the window. I thought of the handsome and clever young man in the field, with his pair of green trousers and suspenders, and of the birds chattering in the silence that followed.

I swelled with pride and conviction, and with determination that I would rekindle those old feelings of chivalry and valour and human dignity which I had heard the old rector speak of in his quiet moments after tea. I imagined that I too could develop some of those chivalrous characteristics, that I too might become a same wartime hero who would rescue the wounded Gordie Gates and pull him across the field in an army stretcher and take him to the pretty nurse for safe-keeping. Then I would hand deliver the news of his safe recovery to a youthful rector. I was soon lost in this feeling of goodness, but when I came down the creaky stairway and approached the old rector while he sat in his study, the gap in our ages and the fear of his reprimand silenced me.

"May I have these, sir?" I said, nervously.

The old man puffed on his pipe.

"What could you possibly want them for, child?"

I had no answer for him. I stared at my toes. The old man sighed. "There are some marvellous hummingbirds in the back garden this year, Selwyn. Blue tits round the delphiniums. Robins in the rose-bushes. Grackles in the trees. What are you interested in, Selwyn?"

I smiled. Twittered like a chaffinch.

"Have them, child," he said.

Every Sunday after church I spied on the prettiest girl in the village, Nancy Mason, who lived in the bungalow across the street. As I watched her in the window, having her hair brushed by her mother, I would imagine her a glorious archangel hovering above me in the clouds, smiling and entreating me to come into her pillowy room where there were chocolates and endless supplies of horlicks and sickly-sweet drinks. When I finally met her in the hall of the school, though, she looked away and trundled on past like a zombie.

Soon I was desperate with frustration, biting my nails to the quick and collecting vegetables in my pockets and staring into the faces of all who passed in utter paranoia. I was convinced that I had developed a staring disorder. That my eyes had glazed over from staring into those binoculars, and that I had become a strange wandering oddity with hollow yellow eyes that shone in my head. Then, after several nights of staring at the ceiling of my bedroom, of casting spells on the little female figurines in family wall hangings, a plump girl named Gertrude Brown appeared like an apparition amongst the sacks of vegetables and fruit on the rectory porch.

"Girl Guide cookies," she announced stiffly. "Fifty cents a box."

I stared at her. She wore dark glasses, had no eyebrows and seemed to glow.

"Are your parents here?" she asked, shifting her weight to her tiptoes.

"Both in bed, sick," I lied. Then I spotted some dark crumbs on her cheeks. I swiped at the crumbs.

"You've been eating the chocolate ones, haven't you?"

Gertrude just stared ahead. A tear pinched out of her eye.

"I won't tell if you don't tell," I said.

Since Gertrude was a well-decorated Girl Guide, she was mortified at the thought of being branded a thief, and so instead of tattling on her I blackmailed her into helping me build a secret castle in the hay barn across the road. This term of servitude was not intended as punishment, but was meant to provide a place of solace and privacy from old people. Though I didn't have much interest in Gertrude other than as a labourer, I soon found that we shared a disdain for noisy parents and teenage menaces on mini-bikes who drove all over the back garden and called you names when you walked home from school. Gertrude soon became fascinated by the hiding-place and I became inflated with my own importance, sitting magisterially on my hay-bale throne. Wearing a crown braided from hay and grass and thistle, I commanded her to disclose all of the little-girl secrets.

1) Did they like boys?
2) Why did they have hard little mosquito spots on their chests?
3) Why did they drop band-aids in their underpants?

But no matter how much I longed to think of Gertrude as a confidante, I could not do so with any passion. Soon I began to obsess about her and the closeness of her and I spent nights staring at the ceiling plotting and scheming how

I could rid myself of her. Finally, after she confessed to me that she was the schoolyard protector of my darling Nancy, I informed her that it was her duty as palace guard to bring all potential suitors for an interview with the palace king. Gertrude became very quiet when she learned of my wish and then she told me that Nancy would never come because she thought I was a nuisance and overly spoiled.

I pleaded and sang songs for Gertrude but she would not budge. Finally, when I brought out a sweet in frustration and plopped it in my mouth, I noticed that Gertrude looked straight at the candy, lovingly.

"What would you give me if she comes?" she asked, inching towards me. I leapt from my seat and told her about an entire tin of prize Christmas jelly babies that I had been hoarding for eight months under my bed and a pack of English sherbets that you couldn't get in Canada and wine gums made from the finest French and Italian wines.

She glared at me and turned her head to the side. I was fearful that she would snub me, and so in a state of wild and fanciful excitement I stood like a ringmaster on the hay bale and barked out a list of things she should have if she complied with my wishes. Two tins of jelly babies. A jar of Christmas figs. Homemade sherbet from the basement freezer. And, from the the very bottom cupboard in the pantry...

"What?" she asked, eyes wide as saucers.

"You'll see," I said, waggling my finger at her.

The next day Gertrude watched me unload my swag on the floor of the hay-bale chambers.

"What is it?" she asked, as I pried open one of the rector's cherished treacle tins with a nail.

"You wouldn't like it," I said, snatching it away and waggling my treacle-dipped finger at her.

It was then I saw her face darken.

The next day my darling Nancy arrived at the mouth of the barn with a barking dachshund on a leash.

Gerty soon tired of manning the entrance of the fort while Nancy and I smooched and so she poked her fat hands through gaps in the hay bales and kicked furiously at the turrets of the castle when we wouldn't acknowledge her. Eventually I crept out and grabbed a length of twine, made a long whip and cracked it on the back of her legs and chased Gerty out of the barn. She relinquished her claim as Officer of the Palace Guard as she lumbered in her woollen skirt into the stalks of corn. But Gerty was a crafty and determined sort. She soon snuck back in through a broken barn door and, brandishing a long plank, pried hay bales from their positions, causing the fort to quake. Soon my dear little Nancy began to cry and shriek in alarm, while the whole fort shook and rattled and that snapping little dachshund sank down to the bottom of the maze of hay bales.

I told Nancy to sit still while I went after that horrid little dog. Nancy sat on a bale like a lump and sobbed pathetically. But things quickly went to hell when I came back up with a terrible hay rash up and down my arms and legs and a neighbouring farmer showed up with a pitchfork and skewered the dog by mistake.

"G'wan now. Git home," said the farmer in green overalls, with the little dog hanging by its collar, squirming and barking. Above us all Gerty perched in the rafters like a giant owl, blinking behind her huge glasses.

"That boy's trouble," she shouted as I kicked my legs high and beat a path back home through a neighbour's rhubarb patch.

Nancy didn't like the cab in the egg truck where we agreed to meet after the palace incident. There were pheasants and birds constantly beating about in the bush above, but I didn't care a sausage. It was all I wanted, a place away from Gerty and the rector and his wife and anyone who would put me to work doing chores around the old rectory. And so we smooched and kissed and touched in that little cramped cab and showed bum in the overturned apple boxes. For the first while I was giddy with excitement about our secretiveness. I ran on about how I wanted to build a small boat and sail down the dirty Cornwallis River and fight the local children and ghosts and Indians that were there and build a very large factory with chocolate and ice lollies to dole out to all the kind children who knew the password to my secret land.

But I soon discovered that Nancy wasn't interested in any of that silly talk; she was too busy fretting about a new coat or bicycle that her father was going to buy for her. While I was patient with her at first, soon I began to feel lonely in her company.

"You don't like me?" she asked one day.

I tried to smile at her, but it was no use.

Soon I was back to ferreting through detective magazines, Enid Blyton books, old Beano comics, any book that I could get my hands on that wasn't a hymn book or a damned sheet of music. Every night at bedtime, the gruff old rector would stand by my bedside and I would look up at him and imagine him a manly colonel in the war with his arms outstretched, sermonizing the dead soldiers who rose from where they lay.

"If not a bedtime psalm, then sing a prayer, Selwyn."

"I'm too tired," I replied, turning in my bed. I closed my eyes. The smell of his tobacco. A flare. A pipe shadow against the wall. I could hear the soft drone of the rector's wife in the hallway.

"Should we tell him tonight, Hugh? He seemed so happy today."

"Tomorrow, Gwendolyn."

"Will he be alright?"

"He'll be fine."

Through the walls and the door, down the stairs, I could hear the rector singing:

Now I lay me down to sleep
Pray the Lord my soul to keep
If I die before I wake
Pray the Lord my soul to take

As I stared at the ceiling, my head began to flood with images and snippets of songs. An arch of limbs. English voices, singing. Oranges and lemons ring the halls of Saint Clement's... ashes to ashes we all fall down...falling, lying there. Cow corn. High stalks of it. Kids playing games. Running and hiding in the maze of seven-foot-high stalks. Singing. You're it, Jesse Chase. I tagged you. You're it. No I'm not. Wuufff. The sound of swinging limbs. Gotcha. Yes you are. You're it. Running. Lawn furniture tumbling. A smack. A terrible pause. An awwwwwww, like a siren. I'm telling maaaawwwwwmmmmm...slower now...a smell. Dank and coldish. The smell of incense. Solemn, solemn. Chanting like monks in a cave. I believe in one holy Catholic and apostolic church, the remission of sins and in the life everlasting... Bright lights through the curtains. Waking up. The rector's wife standing there in the doorway, smiling.

"Rise and shine, Selwyn. Guess what day it is, dear...?" Me rubbing my eyes.

"It's your birthday, dear. We have something very important that we want to give to you."

We all ate breakfast in the scullery. Poached eggs. White toast. Butter, marmalade and tea. There in the hearth of the scullery was a heaping mound of presents. More than I had ever been given. Some of the boxes contained clothing, shorts, socks and underpants with little kites on them. The large one was a cage with what looked like two little bored guinea pigs.

"Rabbits, dear," corrected Gwendolyn.

I looked at Bee. She looked strange to me with her hands behind her back.

"There's one more, Selwyn." She laid the last one tentatively on the table.

"Don't be alarmed, dear," she said, throwing the rector a worried glance.

I looked at a little velvet Bible. Inside was a yellowed news clipping which read

Baby Boy Abandoned

CP—September 24 1963. Penny Creek, Belcher County, N.S.
A tiny baby boy was found late Wednesday night "crying like a tom-cat" in a section of Gravenstein trees at Varney's U-pick, on Smiths road. Local farm-hand Fulton Varney Jr., who was moving bins around his father's farm, discovered the baby tucked into a hockey bag in the middle of a row of Gravensteins. Police and a detachment of the Penny Creek Volunteer Fire Department combed the area late into the night with searchlights looking for clues to see who might have abandoned the child. Few details have been released at the time of reporting but when asked if he was considering adopting the boy, local fire chief and orchard owner Clayton Varney Sr. replied, "My hands are full with Fulton." When pressed to elaborate, Clayton told the Valley Sentinel that his mentally challenged son, who made the discovery, became possessive and unruly when his mother, Anglican Church Women's Treasurer Mildred Varney, tried to wash the abandoned newborn in the sink. Seeing the child in some distress, Mildred called her best friend, Gwendolyn Davis, who sent round her husband, Anglican minister Hugh Davis, to collect him. When the Sentinel contacted the good minister early Thursday morning, he reported that "the parish will protect the child till someone comes round to claim him."

CHAPTER 5

I became terribly depressed after learning that I had been adopted and while I did not hold any resentment towards the rector and Bee, I was confused. I knew that what love I felt from them was true love, but I also knew that there was something in me that felt unsure about whether I loved them back in the same entire and unconditional way. Perhaps it was the shock of the news or perhaps it was my coming into the years known as puberty, but the more I thought about the absurd image of me being left there in the middle of that field, the more I realized the strange and unfortunate turns life can take.

The rector and Bee were very kind to me during this time, and took great pains to tell me that there had been a moratorium in the community on the subject. They said they were telling me against the advice of many who believed I should never be told. They both thought it best for me to face this truth as a child, rather than as an adult who might stumble on the news in a shoebox in the twilight of life. However, no matter the happy nods and comforting smiles at teatime, I felt myself harden as the months passed. For the first time, I found myself wondering why I seemed so unable to have many children friends. And so I focused what remaining love I might have ever felt for human beings on those birthday rabbits, the year that I turned thirteen.

Chapter 6

The male rabbit was a handsome rabbit with a circular black dot on its forehead and little ragged grey patches round its back and hindquarters. I fancied the male rabbit at first and held him tight in my grasp in the back garden and named him Winchester after the rifle that I had read about in a children's reader, *Tales of the Midwest*. The female rabbit, Amanda, was perfectly snow-white, with bright pink eyes which went red like blood.

I soon favoured Amanda over Winchester because Amanda would greet me at the cage and thump her foot when I brought food. I sensed a certain practicality in her behaviour, as if she knew I was coming for her at that exact time every day, and that she was always going to be there in that cage waiting for me no matter what. Sometimes I would take the two rabbits out of the cage and put them in the old stove where we used to dry onions so that I could watch them together, but they would always stare at each other blankly and twitch their noses in a bored manner. Occasionally one of the house cats followed me out through the back and sat on top of the cage and looked down at Amanda, twitching his tail jealously. Bee would come outside with a handful of chard, brush Barney off the top of the cage and ask me if I wanted to breed the rabbits with any of the other children's rabbits down the street. I always solemnly replied, "No." My own two rabbits were all that I wanted for breeding.

Around the first of March I started to grow impatient. Bee had promised that I could breed Winchester and Amanda, keep a pet from the litter and sell the rest of the bunnies for a new push bike. For nearly three weeks I waited in anticipation for Bee to give me the nod, but despite her promises Bee seemed continually preoccupied with church business and always said *tomorrow dear* or *in time dear in time.* The more impatient I became the more annoyed she became in return. The frustration of waiting made my mind start to wander. I envisioned the two rabbits as lovers, Amanda a beautiful courtyard damsel imprisoned in a castle, pining away for her wayward prince, Winchester. Then I imagined the rabbits as my own parents. I saw their quiet noses through the cage and heard the parental chit-chat that they might have had when the light grew dim during the cool spring nights. Finally I could take the expectation no more. When Bee was away visiting one of the sick members of the parish, I stole out to the barn in a pair of gumboots and lifted Winchester into the cage with Amanda. But they did not kiss and nuzzle each other as I hoped they might. I watched in horror as Winchester pounced on Amanda and mounted from the wrong end and started bucking as Amanda's ears drew flat like a cat's. Then Amanda's eyes became stale and her mouth fell open and a terrible squeal rang through the barn:

Screeeeeeeeeeeeeeeeeeeeeeeeeeeeeeeeeeeeeeeeeeeee

The sound was so loud and disturbing I had to cover my ears with my hands. Then I found myself screaming in time with Amanda. I collapsed in the hubbub and when I finally opened my eyes, Winchester was slumped to the side of the cage. To my dismay, my poor little bunny Amanda was staring straight ahead, eyes blood-red and panting.

The next morning the rector's wife told me that the time had come to breed the rabbits, and that I was to go with her into the barn and help her do it. I knew I could not stomach the possibility of that awful din again, so I told her that I was feeling sickly from sitting in the sun room too long. Bee eyed me for a second. "That's very peculiar of you Selwyn," she said, before pulling on her galoshes and making her way out to the rectory barn. From the sitting-room window I watched her go into the barn and saw her take Amanda towards Winchester's cage. I felt a lump in my throat and I raced up the stairs and turned up the volume on the old wireless in the bedroom. I sank into a chair and covered my ears with my hands, trying to shut out the sounds that those rabbits would make.

For nine long weeks I lived in the rectory in a mixture of fear and guilty silence, imagining that Amanda was gobbling every carrot and bit of chard that was put in front of her, slowly inflating into a large vengeful beast who would have my fingers and hands as penance for what I had done to her. Finally I tiptoed into the rectory barn. Instead of seeing my fat white bunny munching on chard, pregnant and pleased as punch to see me, I was met with an awful smell. There in the corner of the cage was Amanda, stiff as a board. Trampled into the wire cage underneath her were four little hairless bunnies.

When I came through the porch, head down, the rector's wife was ready for me.

"What's in the bread bag, Selwyn?" she asked.

When I opened my mouth to answer her my face went white as a sheet. All that came out was that terrible rabbit sound:

Screeeeeeeeeeeeeeeeeeeeeeeeeeeeeeeeeeeeeeeee

Bee was furious. She marched me up to my room where she made me gaze out the window at a dirty group of children fighting in the nearby field.

"Selwyn Davis," she said, "you've simply got to mix with the other kids."

The next day Bee signed me up to play softball with the village kids behind the school. While I resisted passionately and refused to come to dinner for several days, I was secretly relieved. I needed to recover from the trauma of my dead bunnies, and games gave me time during the day to get away from the daily monotony of reading and playing the flugelhorn. Also, and more important to Bee, it forced me to acknowledge, in a kind of surly manner, the village kids.

Because all the infield positions were always taken by the larger kids, I was stuck patrolling the outfield. While I scowled sullenly and played the fool, there was a certain independence and solitude waiting there, and I soon found that I was very good at playing outfield. I could judge the ball as it was arcing over the sky and though my arm wasn't strong, I had dead aim. I would get my bearings, dash forwards and snap the ball closed in my glove. Then I would run a half-step and whip an underhand worm-burner straight to second base. More often than not, the scruffy little terror trying to stretch a single into a double would find himself in a cloud of dust. "Yer out," one of the smaller children would squawk from a bank of sod near the base.

Before long I was familiar enough with these children to accompany them in their ramblings behind the chicken barn where the blackberries grew as large as rosebuds. One of the children was a dark-haired brute, the rogue cousin of one of the locals, I assumed. I was very wary of him because he seemed to be singling me out. I became alarmed when he came right up to me and stood straight and announced that he was none other than Luke Caldwell. I saw in an instant that this handsome horse was the same whiny pipsqueak that I had known in nursery school. I could see it in his eyes and in his confident grace and in the way the other children bandied around him. We'd had little interaction since I'd sent him tearing into the cow corn years before, but I soon realized that he still harbored ill-feelings towards me. He was watching me where I stood awkwardly at the backstop, swatting at balls that were lobbed towards me. I knew that as much as I tried not to acknowledge the taunts, I was terrified of this little twerp. My eyes were closed the whole time I was at bat.

"Selwyn," he said, stalking me in the brambles, "dare you to eat a berry with a spit bug on it."

I stared at him. "I will not."

"Why not? No one will like you if you don't."

"Don't care."

"Do too."

"Don't care."

"Do too."

And so it went. Luke's voice became a siren for all the hates and biles that lived in the hearts of those little miseries and soon a mean circle of children aged three to ten gathered round as I stared at the berry with the white froth on its stem.

"Do it."

"Eat it."

The whole street began to chant and clap its hands together:

"Do it."

"Eat it."

"Now."

I deposited the blackberry into my mouth and chewed on it till it was gone. Then the chanting changed to:

"You-ate-my-spi-i-it!"

"You-ate-my-spi-i-it!"

"You-ate-my-spi-i-it!"

Luke was soon bragging in a singsong voice. He dribbled spit into the palm of his hand, his eyes wide open. "Anybody else want to eat my spit? Huh?"

All the little kids and some of the bigger ones too, they shook their heads.

"Nooooooo."

For a second I saw nothing, thought nothing, just froze there on the spot. Then:

Screeeeeeeeeeeeeeeeeeeeeeeeeeeeeeeeeeeeeeeee

I stood there with my hands over my ears and belted out a pure one-note squeal so potent in its release that the dogs outside the chicken barn began to yelp and bellow and the village kids had to cover their ears with their hands. When I opened my eyes their eyes were bonded shut and their hands were gripping the sides of their heads. The whole time that I had been screaming I was overwhelmed with the most frightful thoughts. Of buzzing planes and dropping buzz bombs and an electric sky. Of two giant violin bows sawing a man to bits. Of those horrid Siamese cats eating old Miss Jess in the rectory scullery, and finally of the terrible unsettling sight of Amanda and Winchester rutting.

When I opened my eyes I knew that I could never be like the other happy children. When I bowed demonstrably towards them they all turned towards me and sang like choir-boys:

> "Christmas pageant...Christmas pageant...Christmas pageant."

I lifted my arms and beat my wings and flew after them like a giant seagull. But they took to the brambly hills. Fled.

A month later the rector asked me to sing an aria during Communion, knowing full well that I hated singing in public. The old rector knew nothing of my episode with the village children. I was to memorize "O Lamb of God" and sing it as the lead soprano with the choir as the congregation filed up the aisle towards the altar during the offertory hymn. Instead of arguing with him, I took my place in the choir, wearing a special purple gown. I waited as they hummed:

Oh Lamb of God
That takest away the sins
of the world
Have mercy upon us
Have mercy upon us

Everyone in the congregation, including the rector, who was pouring wine from his chalice, turned to look with pride at the adopted son with the perfect pitch. I cleared my throat, relaxed my vocal chords and stared up at the ceiling-fan. All I saw and heard were those two rabbits:

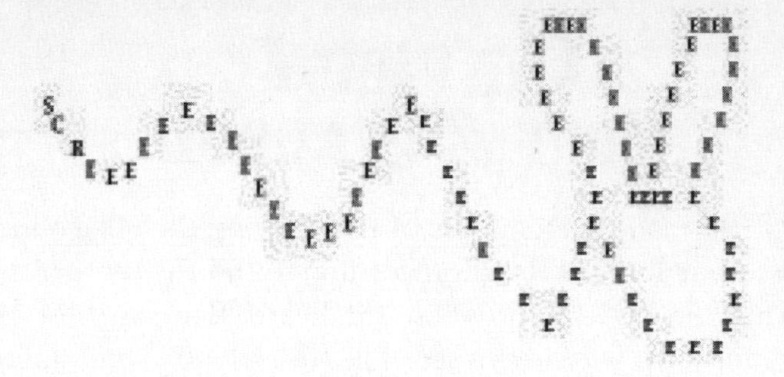

The congregation gasped at the sound. And a red stain spread like a gunshot wound across the rector's white Communion cassock.

Chapter 7
Jerry O'Reardon

Since I had made such a mess of befriending the village kids, I didn't want Jerry O'Reardon coming round the rectory and pestering me, especially when I'd heard Bee say that the immigrant boy was heavy-set, far too friendly and talked sport in a trembling voice that went up two octaves when he was nervous. But I soon warmed to Jerry when he escaped from the rector's tight grasp, clambered on top of the bingo table, fought with the green and orange streamers which dangled from the Penny Creek Fire Hall and roared with red cheeks: "Feel welcome do I? I feel like I been marooned." Bingo blotters stopped. Lit cigarettes dropped into paunches. The immigrant boy had just insulted the villagers.

And so because none of the old church women liked the look of him and the village kids were little Huns to him at the tea reception at the fire hall, Jerry, his mother and sullen brother shuttled out through the dingy stairwell and assembled in a dreary cluster under an umbrella in the parking lot.

"Should we do something for them, Hugh?" asked Bee when we all got back to the rectory that evening.

"The Baptists will see to them," said the rector, puffing on his pipe in the sitting-room.

"Selwyn," said Bee, hunting me down in the larder, "you need a little chum."

"No I don't," I answered, scarfing cheese in the larder. I kept my head down and bolted up the stairs.

I hid from Jerry whenever I saw him at village functions during the stifling heat of August, but fate has always been cruel to me, and when September came round the fat lug was stuck in the same homeroom as me. The teacher, Mr. Darbeson, took one look at Jerry, settled there into the middle of the class in his neatly pressed fourth-form Irish school uniform, and dropped his chalk to the floor.

"Will we sing the anthem then, sir?" asked Jerry. Moon face. Middle of the row like a green stain.

"What anthem, Jerry?" said Darbeson.

"The school anthem, sir."

"Stand against the wall, young man."

Jerry stood, fat legs dimpling. "Way, Sir? I in't don nothing." The teacher mulled. Turned surly.

"Recite "Oh Canada" for the class, please." Jerry laughed uncomfortably and then started to frown.

"I dunno sir."

"Your anthem then please, Jerry. For the class."

Darbeson waited while the largest kid in the class, his hands like coal-shovels, blew his nose like a trumpet. Jerry stood feet together at the front of the class. He started to tremble.

"The North County school anthem is what I know, sir."

"Fine. Start please."

Jerry began to warble:

> The gawlden cackrel craws in the morning.
> Wake up children welcome the day...

At recess the kids circled like crows over a freshly tilled cornfield.

"Git away wi' yer," said Jerry, kicking at them all with his fat legs.

Jerry was crying after school and came after me like a shot. He told me all about his Sunday newspapers that he used to plug up holes in the school toilet and when you took them away there was a wee hole you could look through and see the teachers smoking even though they said they didn't. I soon broke into a trot but Jerry stayed with me, telling me that he hated animals with a passion though he had made an exception for a Jack Russell terrier that his mother had imported all the way from Belfast. I looked at his fat fingers stretching for me.

"I hate dogs, especially small ones," I told him as I lunged away from those fat fingers.

"Caim down yah bennie," Jerry roared, drop-kicking an ear of cow corn onto a neighbour's immaculately trimmed hedgerow.

The fat bastard followed me all the way down to the bottom of the lane and talked so much about his horrid dog that I told him I would never go by to visit while the dog was alive. But Jerry was a persistent sod and before the week was out I was a bored and lonely stiff in the doorway of the crummy little apartment where he lived. When we got past the beer bottles and cigarettes in the portico, I was into the living-room, which smelled of smoke.

"Sherry's a love," said his mother, standing in her dressing-gown and dragging on a smoke.

"You have a daughter?" I asked.

A dark nose poked through a blanket. A yip. A sudden terrifying yip and that damned dog sprang from the sofa, stared at me with little mean eyes and nipped me hard when I lowered my hand to pet it.

"Ah, he's not so bad," Jerry's mother, Bernice, confided, petting the thing. "He jus' smells a bit a cat on ye is all."

Jerry threw the dog into the basement, locked the door and told his mother to put his brother to bed. He then took me straight into his room where we sat on an unmade bed. Jerry stared right into me.

"I don't like it here," he said. "The villagers are drips and they say bad things." Jerry stood on tiptoes, handed me a photo.

"Jarge O'Reardon. Me da'." He combed his hair over. "The day I turn seventeen I'm chartering a plane to Belfast to avenge his death."

"What happened to him?"

"Strangled in jail by a Bretish saldier."

Jerry drew close. I could feel his breath on me.

"Brets. Only good fer one thing."

"What, Jerry?" I asked, not understanding a word.

"Sexy birds on telly. Yew like them then?" Jerry pointed at

the stacks and stacks of *Gent* and *Mayfair* magazines that were thrown in a beaten suitcase on the floor. I hummed and flipped.

"I'm bared. You bared, Selwyn?"

I nodded, eyes glued to the pages.

"Look out the way, then." Jerry stabbed his arm far under the bed and dragged a shabby box across the room. Inside was an ugly grey metal thing that looked like a bomb. Or a gun. Jerry squatted and started to tinker with it. He peered up at me. Hair all over his red face. "Yah have past pewberty, then?"

I blinked in the darkness as he drew the blinds. We then sat like two pigeons on the edge of the bed. There was an uncomfortable silence. Then a whirring and clacking. There on the grimy blinds before us two tall blond women in heavy makeup slapped at each other while a man with bushy hair and sideburns grinned.

Jerry shifted in his seat. I gawked at him. "Soon as the balls drop, yer away," he said.

Jerry fumbled with the string of his satiny blue Umbro shorts. One hand twisted the projector focus button. He turned and yelled at me.

"Well come on then. Punch it Salwyn!!"

I gave it a go.

"But it hurts!" I cried.

"Look a' them two blond tarts, Salwyn," Jerry was grimacing and gasping and pointing, "look at them big sweaties."

We sat like blinking peafowl and did the business.

"Tissyew, Salwyn," he screeched, "you're not gaina use the tissyew, then?"

Unimpressed, embarrassed, exhausted, I grunted, "I'm going home."

It was carnage the whole year. We killed pigeons in the barn, shot at passing bicyclists with Jerry's BB gun, fished for tommy cod in the Cornwallis River, stuck firecrackers in the asses of live frogs, threw rotten chicken eggs at houses down the street, set the Gaspereau Bridge on fire, drove the farmer's tractor into a ravine and bragged about the number of times in one day we had wacked off, pushing each other to more ridiculous limits until finally his obsession with soccer and Georgie Best and all things Irish made me hate him as much as the other kids. But stay with him I did, for Jerry had the charm, and as much as I wanted to run for the hills from him, I could not. The bastard made me laugh till my guts split.

Chapter 8

If we were ever short of money and the bugger couldn't steal money from his ma's change purse or pawn a plate or dish from the barn behind the rectory he'd tell me that I had my hands in my pockets far too much and if we had our wits about us we'd both be living in mansions at the top of the lane. Then it'd be that nervous voice and my heart would sink and he'd call over to the old lady raking chestnuts into an orange garbage bag across the way.

"I'll bet it aches yer legs and back bendin' down over that pile a wet leaves and black conkers. What yew need with that lovely lawn is a gardener, Miss Wallace. Salwyn knows a bit about chores, don't yah then?" Jerry nudged me. "Why don't you ask him about it?"

"No, Jerry," I hissed, "I hate doing chores."

Jerry pinched me and whispered. "Wouldcha just go along with it, Sally boy? If she pays us up front we can get a coopla dirty magazines and a can er two a cheep beer and sit under the bridge and throw rocks at pigeons fer the afternoon."

"I don't want to throw rocks at pigeons."

He gripped my hand, hard. Stared at me. "Why not then yah soft-hearted little bennie. What else we gaina do?"

"Is that you, the naughty Davis child?" The old lady across the street rattled her walker and blinked.

"Aye, that's him alright," called Jerry. His faced knifed forwards. "That's the lazy bastard who won't give an old nag like you a hand."

Jerry took my hand and we hopped on the back of my bike and straddled it and peddled like the clappers all the way home.

We hid in the basement of rectory. Jerry lit his Bic lighter while I tried to find the light switch in the dark.

"That was an easy tenner, Selwyn. Could you not do it for half a day, then?"

I shook my head. "Would you?"

"No I wouldn't yah blue-faced little fairy, but I'm the broker in't I? The broker's the one that takes the money. Fifty parcent."

I found the switch. Jerry looked around, wide-eyed. "Jesus Selwyn. What the hell do you do down here anyway? Grow potatoes and mould? Have you a record player or even a stereo? What about some ABBA or Carpenter music?"

"Music?" I pulled a record from a milk crate and presented it to him.

"*Peter and the Wolf*? Jeesus, Salwyn. I'm talkin about Bee Gees. Gloria Gaynor. You don't listen to music then?"

"I play it," I replied.

"What, rock guitar?"

"No, the flugelhorn."

"The fluggelharn! Is that why yew hide away in this old rectory most the time? 'Cause you're in a secret marching band?"

"I used to play in the high-school band."

"Didjah new?" Jerry's eyes widened. "Didjah play any poplar music in the school band? Any Carpenters music? Lovely music Carpenter music."

"No."

"Bucks Fizz?"

"What?"

"Yew dainno Bucks Fizz? Back home I used to watch Bucks Fizz with my younger brother on Top the Pops, Frayday nights. Me da', before he dayd, bring home a paint a' cider and pour me and Kieran a little glass before he was away to play cards with Denny O'Brien and Seamus O'Sea down the Salty Bird. Bu' Bucks Fizz, Salwyn. Every kid I know had a strobe light and danced the silly dance wanted a British bird like the Bucks Fizz birds. Blond hair and shart sharts. They won the Euro song contest two yars back."

"What's that?"

"Ne'er you mind, yah daft cunt." Jerry stood up and brushed himself off.

"Yew must know traditional music, Salwyn. What about "Danny Boy"? What about Vera Lynn? "The White Cliffs of Dover"? Jesus you play "The White Cliffs of Dover" and me mum'll rent a piano straight away and start singin'."

"I know "Farewell to Nova Scotia"," I said. I put the mouthpiece to my lips and started to play it.

"Gawd," Jerry covered his ears, "that's a tarrible song, Selwyn. TARRIBLE. Something we both know. Something international. The Muppets. Everybody knows the theme song to the Miss Piggy and Kermit show."

I did know it. I knew it from a school band competition and so in the gloom of that dark cellar I pressed my lips to the mouthpiece of the flugelhorn and began to play.

Dah dah dah dah dah dah dah
dee dee dee dee dee dee
duh duh duh duh duh duh duh
It's time to get things started
Why don't you get things started
On the Muppets Show Tonight

Jerry found a pile of giant margarine tubs, then took a pair of the rector's gumboots, emptied the straw out of them and drubbed like an animal on the tops of those tubs.

Very soon after that Jerry and I weren't speaking to one another. He had abandoned me in the middle of a mucky soccer pitch and left me standing there with my socks round my ankles and round red welts on both thighs, nursing my shins, which he had hacked to bits. Then the bugger stole my bike off the pitch and called me a "lazy tit" and biked straight down the lane and over the village bridge and across the dyke land into the town, where he pasted an advertisement in the local convenience store that said he was looking for a mate to train with and had an extra pair of trainers and a full kit of top-rung Adidas gear. When I came in that night the rector was in the sitting room, puffing. He coughed once.

"Where were you lad?"

"Out with Jerry, sir."

I looked hard at the old man. He coughed again, tried to

joke. “If bennies were pennies then that young fool’s made his mint.” The rector coughed again.

“Sit down Hugh,” said Bee, coming in. She lingered over him. “Will you just sit down, Hugh?” The old man coughed again. He looked sick. “Selwyn,” he called after me, “we need to talk.”

But I just loped up the stairs thinking hard about Jerry O’Reardon and that push bike he’d nipped, and I pretended I hadn’t heard a word that the old rector had said to me.

Chapter 9

The spring of 1978 was a sad year. The rector was diagnosed with advanced cancer of the colon. The polyps in his bowels blew up the size of small balloons and it was a dismal part of the day when he went to the bathroom. The sound he made was deafening, grunting and gasping as he did, occasionally humming church hymns in embarrassment lest one of his parishioners should come by and visit him at his lowest ebb. I always seemed to have the misfortune of coming into the house when the old man was on the throne and so I made a habit of loitering in the rectory barn with the cats and the chickens hoping that he would get up and back to his sickbed safely himself. But of course he never did and the Bee was always there to sternly instruct me to "take care of the loo" while she got him back to bed.

The pain of seeing her husband shrink away soon took its toll on Bee, and this was most evident in the way she treated him when he was lying in the bed. Sometimes she would be quietly amused by something the old Rector might say and tease him about how handsome he was with a scruff on his beard. But I would catch her in her private moments, staring off blankly, whispering to herself while she vacuumed the house for the fifth time, or sniffling on the phone telling old Mrs. Varney that if he had had more check-ups and had turfed that awful pipe this easily could have been prevented.

My feelings towards the rector were equally mixed. I was fifteen years old and had no interest in the grim prospect of nursing an old man through his dying days. Still, I relented to the pressure, and attended to him without complaint because I felt a stubborn and proud sense of loyalty to this old man who had welcomed me into the Davis family so unconditionally. As the time went by, I grew used to the horrors of bedpans and long empty stares. I stood by his bedside and silently watched him die. I knew in my gut that I had disappointed him greatly by not living up to my early musical promise. I sat alone with him in the dark of night and savoured the wise and thoughtful things he told me of his life as a young man. I knew that I was clinging to him. The simple grim truth of the matter was that I was closer to this old man than I was to any other male figure in my life.

Within a year, the rector was down to nine and a half stone. Four months later, the day before his seventy-fifth birthday, he was dead. The day he passed, Bee came calmly into the sitting-room where I was reading and told me to run hot water in a basin. She told me that he had passed away in the few moments prior and that I was not to be alarmed and was to fetch his washing kit from the bathroom cupboard. When I came into the bedroom, I sat there at her side, while she meticulously lathered and then shaved the old man's stubble from his face for the last time.

"There you are my love," she said as she smoothed his cheek with her arthritic hand. She brushed his hair from the top of his head and leaned down and kissed him on the temple. She turned towards me.

"Is there anything that you want to say to him, Selwyn?"

I held Bee's hand and hugged her and then eased off the bed and went into my room and collected my old black flugelhorn case. We sat side by side very calmly and silently. I played while she sang in a whispery but stunningly clear voice:

The sun shall not smite you by day
nor the moon by night
The Lord will keep you from all evil
he will keep your life

The old rector was buried in a plot behind the church cemetery. His obituary appeared on the sixth page of the *Halifax Chronicle Herald.*

WAR VETERAN AND ANGLICAN MINISTER HUGH DAVIS DEAD AT 75

Hugh Davis was born on a small farm in

Oxfordshire in 1903. The last in a line of eight sons, he was educated at prestigious Coke Thorpe School, and took his Master of Divinity at Keble College, OXON. In 1939 he was conscripted into the war and soon rose to the position of Sergeant-Major. In 1942 he commanded an Allied force in Paris, France, where he was injured in a bombing. In 1943 he was captured by German troops while showering in a Dutch cottage, and, mistaken for a hiding Pole, was taken to an internment camp. It was there that he managed to convince the authorities that he was English, but was still forced to stay there until after the war. He was instrumental in leaking information about the hardships and depraved conditions in the camp, and reached national fame when he appeared as a guest on *Front Page Challenge* in 1979. He is survived by his wife Gwendolyn and an adopted son, Selwyn, 15.

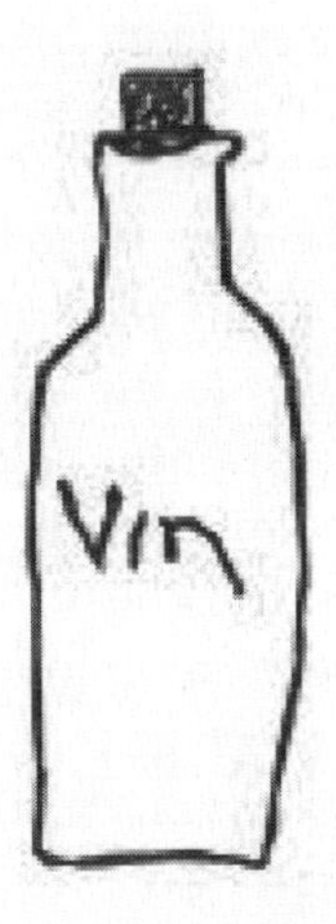

Chapter 10

With the rector gone and Bee's eyesight failing her, I hit the bottle at sixteen. I became a demon for cheap white wine, which I bought for $4.75 a litre at the liquor commission on Main Street in the local town. It wasn't hard to get. Bee lent me the parish car, so on Friday nights I would tell her that I was going to deliver the church newsletter to some of the sick and feeble members of the parish. Instead I would park the car in the back of the liquor commission, grab two bottles of cheap sparkling wine and pay for it with the ten bucks that I got for allowance. Since I looked older than I was and dressed in work clothes from the rectory barn, I never got asked for identification.

Most weeks after school was out I drove the rectory car behind the old chip factory. I would sip from the bottle and sit there contented and pacified, letting the slow glow of the buzz wash over me. I wasn't melancholy so much as I was dipsy. It seemed as I sat and drank that I was in truth a lonely child, but lonely in a way that I had chosen to be. Very soon I found that I was crying and that crying was what felt so good and settling to me. After some time sitting there and drinking and crying for the loss of the old man and the knowledge that I had never really made my peace with him, I started the car and took one of the back roads and parked the car in the laneway outside the rectory. When I got back into the scullery, I ate a spoonful of peanut butter and gave the rector's wife the remaining copies of the church newsletters. I kissed her once on the cheek.

"Thank you dearie," she said, collecting them into a pile that she fastened with a piece of twine.

"Mrs. Betts happy to see you dear?" Bee called as I made my way back out the porch again.

"Oh yes," I answered, pulling the porch door closed. I then drove blind drunk to the hockey game.

I went to the arena every week because I was in awe of the athleticism of the teenage boys who had the confidence and coordination to make the team. Luke Caldwell was the team captain. Jerry O'Reardon soon signed up, for a laugh. Adept at kicking the puck between his skates, Jerry was mired in nets because he couldn't skate. The rest of the high-school team was made up of a ragged crew of jocks from the South Mountain who could skate like the wind but couldn't afford proper hockey equipment. One of them was a red-headed beast with a big nose who went by the name of "Big Garfield". He was a target for all the fast little men on the ice because he was two hundred pounds and couldn't skate backwards. It was a well-kept secret that Big Garfield hid cardboard in the padding of his cheap Home Hardware hockey gear, but the truth leaked out one Friday night when the inside section of a Stapleton's Apple Sauce box dropped through a hole in his hockey pants. The opposing player took one look at the box and started to pass the cardboard around the ice like a puck. Garfield took the boy's stick, broke it on the ice and started waving the sharpened frayed ends at the player.

"Get 'im, Garfield. Get 'im." His mother, dressed in a flowing tent, stood at the glass near the ice and bellowed.

The games were played at the old university rink in the town. The rink was a cavernous, poorly-lit building with huge pillars rising upward through the stands. The pride of the building, the university's Zamboni, rarely worked, and so a tractor was donated by one of the local dairy farmers, who drove the groaning old thing around the ice between periods dragging a sodden towel. A couple of rink rats wearing navy blue university jackets would frequently scamper onto the ice and shovel snow off the surface, then take their spots again in the penalty box, where they doubled as timekeepers.

In the stands, the prettiest and most popular girls would cozy together in their boyfriends' hockey jackets near the home-team bench. The rest of the town's schoolteachers, mechanics, morticians, hairdressers and university professors huddled near a thick white support pillar and gossiped to one another during the course of the game. After a couple of false starts, seated beside older men who seemed determined to commiserate with me about the rector's sudden death, I settled on a private spot high up in the stands at the end of the rink. I was behind the time clock, above the canteen. I took a lawn chair, covered myself with a blanket and made myself at home. From my solitary and safe position up above the rink, I took the rector's old military telescope and scanned the crowd.

CHAPTER 11

In my bid to find comfort for my loneliness I now determined to find a female confidante. I was through with boys and men. My reasoning was simple. Jerry had done a bunk on me and the only person I trusted in my life, now that the old rector had died, was female—Bee. However, since most of the girls in my year were out to get me (Gertrude Brown had once sent a pack of her friends after me, hissing like geese), I set my sights on the only logical choice, Charlene Lockhart, a fidgety transfer student who was sequestered in maths tutorials late after school. The competition was not fierce for her interests. She had a few odd habits and the rumour amongst the jocks and brutes in the smoking section of the school was that she was peculiar.

I was mad for Charlene because she was nervous like me and had a tendency to count with her fingers in her palm and fidget. She was also a first-rate stunner, with black hair, a large bosom, high bottom and long thin legs like a dancer. Every Friday night I would gaze at her with my binoculars and marvel at the peculiarity of this beautiful young woman stabbing her hands by her sides, looking for something she had lost.

She was exactly the type of girl I wanted. I soon became obsessed with her. I sat there and made notes about her habits, wondering how she spoke, imagining the clever and intriguing conversations we might have. I imagined that she would sit with her cap on her head and say the same silly things as me, and that we would hold hands and titter and kiss and there would never be that awful expectation to say something clever or highly meaningful.

However, because I had been blacklisted by the boys in the school and was public enemy number one to Gertrude Brown and her ilk, I had to plot my introduction to her carefully. I was resolved not to mess this up, and so I staked out my territory in that hockey rink and waited patiently above the time clock till the second intermission, when all the pretty girls in Charlene's crowd rose like members of the church congregation and made their way towards the canteen. I nearly did a burton as I waited up there. There were some scorchers in Charlene's crowd. But I only had eyes for Charlene.

"You want a hot dog, Charlene?" Vivian, elegant, sharp-featured, remarked.

"Hot dog?" Charlene looked up, suddenly. Smiled.

"Yes. We're all getting dogs. Would you like one?"

"Yes, one dog..."

A hand at a wrist. "What did you forget, Charlene?"

"My scarf, Vivian? I can't find it."

"It's around your neck, Charlene."

"My barrette. Seen that?"

Viv grabbed a curl of that black hair.

"This barrette, Char?"

"Oh, silly goose."

Above them I sat in a lawn chair I had brought from home, staring down at the shiny black hair cascading over Charlene's shoulders, her pink neck, warm and soft and shadowy. There I was like the town drunk with a blanket over my legs, leaning down over the bannister. Brandishing a little pocket radio, I sang along to a tune that was playing on the radio:

Come on down to my place woman, we make love...

But as soon as Charlene looked around I shrank away like a child that has thrown a snowball at a moving car and the car has stopped and a vengeful-looking man has stepped out.

Chapter 12

Charlene only became more attractive as the year passed. But I hadn't the courage to approach her. I would spot her at the school dance looking bemused and standing slightly away from her crowd of friends. Then, just as I was about to brace myself for a charge through the crowds to interview her, some lustful cow in a patterned dress would take the corner and pin me there.

"Selwyn Davis you look lonely standin' there. My guess is you want to dance."

"Dance?"

"You know. Shake your hips. Sway to the music."

"You make me want to vomit," I would reply.

Then, while reflected light glided around the walls of the gymnasium, I would be dragged out to the dance floor and bear-hugged for the duration of the slow dance. While we rotated uncomfortably, a crowd of teenage matrons, each with a similar teenage wastrel crushed into her chests, nodded approvingly from the side. When the song was done I pried myself free and backed into a corner.

"Don't come another step closer to me," I said.

There was an inching forwards of intrigued fems. Pink and deliciously hostile faces.

"Just one more. I'm not going to hurt you, Selwyn."

"I told you no."

Just then, another one, with drab jeans and straight greasy black hair, raised her hand towards me, like a mummy.

"No!"

"Just one dance."

More inching forwards.

"You've had it," I mouthed, my fingers in my ear holes:

Screeeeeeeeeeeeeeeeeeeeeeeeeeeeeeeeeeeeeeeee

"He's so weird," one of them would console, wrapping her arms around the girl.

Of course this behaviour would not do and the next day, the guidance counsellor, Mr. Ellerton, summoned me while I stood in the school hallway with a string of muttering dimwits who were about to file into a maths class. I was relieved to be taken from the line because there was a rumour circulating that we were going to be sprung a maths quiz. This tall pleasant man who smiled at me in the hallway of the school represented deliverance from a test I would surely fail. But when I came into his office I was surprised to be greeted by the rector's wife and a burly bald man who resembled an eagle.

For a very long time Bee and the guidance counsellor sat with me. Bee held my hand as I listened to the deliberate and solemn voice of the school principal, who was out to get me. As I sat stone-faced in that room, I listened in surprise to the unwavering voice of a sixty-eight-year-old woman who spoke of me in a very proud way.

"There are those who think he belongs in a special school," said the baldie, Mr. Cankerton.

"Please, Harold." Bee fussed with the hemline of her skirt. "It would be a crime to send him away. He is just sensitive and has an active mind."

"Why should the school make an exception?"

"He's just misunderstood, Harold."

"So are many other truants and delinquents."

Bee stood like a giant owl. "He has love in his heart. He's had a tough time." She looked at me, paused for a second. "Do you know his history?"

The principal turned surly and growled, "I do."

At the end of the meeting it was determined that given the time I was spending in detention for being rude or for shrieking, if I were to stay in school, I was to seek counselling with a child psychiatrist. Bee was concerned, naturally.

"What if this experience worsens him, Harold?" she asked, as she flipped through the list of indiscretions and incidences of rudeness the principal had compiled.

"A shame," said the eagle, "but he's got no choice."

I hated the thought of going for counselling. After the first session, a terrible experience where Dr. Binney sat in a chair while I was forced to speak at length, I ran in tears into the arms of the Bee, who waited patiently for me in the waiting-room.

"Must I go?" I pleaded.

"Don't whine, Selwyn," she said, "it's unbecoming."

Just as the rector's wife and I walked into the elevator, my very darling Charlene came charging out of the thing holding a calculator. She walked straight into my chest, head down, counting.

"Charlene!" her mother gasped.

Afterwards we found ourselves in the hallway between the canteen and the gymnasium. Charlene grabbed my arm and ushered me outside. We sat underneath the school bleachers amongst chocolate bar wrappers, milkshake cartons and wads of discarded gum. Charlene clipped her hair with her barrette.

"So what are you, Selwyn? Obsessive? Compulsive? Neurotic? Hysterical?"

I tried not to stare down her blouse. I thought for a moment.

"Pervert I guess."

"Does anybody know?"

"Know?"

"Know that you go to a psychiatrist?"

"A few teachers, the guidance counsellor, the rector's wife."

"Like me," she said, her voice far away. Then she laughed again, hand at her mouth. Then she looked at me and I was fearful for the first time.

"Selwyn," she gripped my hand hard, then rattled off: "What's your favourite food? What's your favourite chocolate bar? What's your favourite time of the day? What's the best vacation spot...?"

I thought for a moment. "Kraft dinner. Mr. Big. Lunchtime. Turkey?"

"All concerning food. Brilliant," she said. "Want to go out with me on Friday?"

"Where?"

"Town," she replied, counting on her first three fingers, "the old pool."

The recess bell rang. Clangggggggggggggg.

She pressed the fourth finger down and looked at me. "Swimming," she finished.

Chapter 13

The old pool was the smaller of the two pools in the university gymnasium and was rarely used. It was easy to get to, because Charlene had an uncle who worked as a commissionaire on staff and he used to let her in the nights that he worked the late shift. Charlene had her Bronze Medallion, which satisfied some of my immediate concerns about inhaling water instead of air. She could save me if I started to drown and she knew the proper technique for mouth-to-mouth resuscitation. The pool hurt my eyes when I got in, but it wasn't my cries of agony that got Charlene's attention, it was the bottle of Cold Duck that I had in my hand.

"You can't take that into the pool," gasped Charlene.

"Oh," I replied, bobbing up and down, strugging to get hold of the side. The bottle banged against the pool. I dumped the contents into the pool.

Charlene was swimming towards me, taking wide sweeping breaststrokes, her eyes outlined by blue swimming goggles.

"You didn't..."

"Yes I fucking did," I said, my red chlorinated eyes burning.

"You're crazy, Selwyn Davis." Her hair a wet billowing dark storm.

"So are you," I protested.

We kissed underwater.

After the swim I sat near the pool and towelled off while Charlene bounced up and down on the diving board.

"I-love-Selwyn-Davis. I-love-Selwyn-Davis. I-love-Selwyn-Davis," she sang.

"Who's he?" I grimaced, staring at the empty bottle of white wine.

"Very funny," she replied with a scowl. She dove in, came towards me.

"You. You. You. You. You. You," she counted on her fingers, below me.

"One date and you love me? C'mon, Charlene."

"Connections," she said, "don't you believe in connections, Selwyn?"

"Connections? Sounds like some middle-aged dating service, Charlene."

"He's so witty..." Her face to the side. That finger counting again. "And so mean. Why are you so mean, Selwyn?"

"I just say what I think."

"No one will like you, Selwyn."

"No one does, anyway."

Charlene was smiling. She lowered herself down into the water, hair falling back down over her shoulders. She pulled down the strap of her bathing suit. Wriggled herself down lower. Then she smiled in that crazy goofy way. I was all of lost in her as she wriggled her suit down lower. Two red watery suns. White. Wet triangle of black bush.

"C'mon, Selwyn."

I dropped back in and nursed on those nipples like an infant. She held my head.

"Well I like you, you cuckoo."

Chapter 14

The worst part was Charlene couldn't stop thinking of me and I couldn't stop thinking of her. We'd be together all day and then on the phone at night talking, talking, talking. Sometimes, when we were kissing each other, I would fantasize, biting her and sucking on her skin, that it would all just end. We were hopeless. Totally neurotic with each other, wild in the way that young people can be. I became hopelessly lost in her, lost in the safety of the smell of her, lost in her shirt where I would kiss her neck. I could feel a transformation taking place. I could feel the quiet tremors of growing up and I hated those tremors desperately- the responsibility, the pressure of being recorded in photographs, of being polite and courteous in public when I wanted only to be alone with Charlene.

However, while we supported each other and I knew that I loved her, our relationship soon regressed into a kind of melancholy. First she started to talk like me, to pick up tics and little nuances in the way that I spoke, the way I stressed certain words. She'd insist that I imitate people we knew: that fat bastard, Jerry O'Reardon, Bee, school teachers, like Mr. Darbeson, whom we both despised. There'd be a certain giddy anxiety when she asked these things, as if I was in some way reassuring her that other people had their own crosses to bear, worse and more alarming than my own curt tongue and that obsessive finger counting of hers.

As I drank more and more she, of course, started to get in on the bottle too. And as we became closer, her ties with her old girlfriends like Viv began to dissolve, so that by the time we entered grade eleven we were two people who couldn't get enough of each other and couldn't get away from one another. We drank too much and held each other close and drove to remote places where we would just sit together in the car and talk and pull the clothes off each other and bite and kiss each other in forbidden places. We'd try to do all the things that other people did, smile and talk to parents and older people, but the truth of the matter was that we were happiest when we were alone, intoxicated by ourselves. And though we took every precaution against it, the inevitable happened, on the eve of Charlene's seventeenth birthday.

"Selwyn," she said, standing in the doorway and glowing and gasping in a way that scared the hell out of me, "I think. I think. I think I've failed the rabbit test."

Chapter 15

The Rector's wife was against a rush marriage and for having the baby and made her decision promptly and without a lecture. She'd been through this before, decades prior when this whole topic was truly taboo. While she didn't approve, she was resigned to what had happened, resigned to finding a solution to the problem of a surprise grandchild. But Marlene, Charlene's mother, was devastated by what had happened and wouldn't let me come over to her house. She abruptly stood on the old porch and announced to the rector's wife that I had lost her trust and had taken advantage of her deeply troubled daughter. When I tried to patch things up, arriving one day with some flowers picked from the rectory garden, she closed the door in my face. I heard her yelling at me from inside the house as I walked down the lane towards the rector's car. I tried saying that I was sorry, in fact I even tried calling her on the telephone a few times, but noticed that the old cheery message on her machine had been erased and replaced with a cold voice that betrayed a hint of menace. *I am not here to take your call. Please leave a message.*

Charlene was pulled from the high school and gave birth to a baby boy named Hector, after Maureen's father, an apple farmer who had once worked the gypsum boats all over the southern United States. I am told the little boy had Charlene's brown eyes and my dimpled chin and weighed six pound seven ounces in diapers. But I never even got a chance to meet my son or hug Charlene or make a peace with her mother. One night, the darkest night I'll ever remember, Maureen packed Charlene into a car with Hector and the baby seat and pointed the car south towards Arizona to be with her extended family, away from the boy's crazy father. When I drove over the Gaspereau South Mountain I knew that they were gone. The driveway was empty, the house was still, the clothesline was barren and the wind behind blew soft rustles through the cow corn in the fields.

As I drove back home I saw the smoke rising up behind the bluff road in behind the town of Wooval. The sky was blood-red, violet, orange, and I knew as I looked over my shoulder and saw the smoke billow and heard the fire sirens that my life in this town was doomed.

Chapter 16

When the police had left and the detectives finally accepted that I would never admit to burning down that house, I walked into my bedroom, locked the door and fell to pieces completely. I listened to several stern warnings from Bee to the effect that though she fully believed I had not set fire to that house, there had been a saddening deterioration in my morals, and she was beginning to lose faith in me. She spoke to me in a dismissive tone, but she begam leaving "uplifting" books on the end of my bed though I would remain under the covers till she was gone. After a while I began picking through what she left in the room for me—copies of *Guideposts*, a hardcover book: *God's Firm and Resolute Hand*, *Reader's Digest*, *Crossword Today*, old *Life* magazines and *National Geographics*. Somewhere in that month of loneliness and lying in bed, I found the old flugelhorn and began playing it again as if there were no notes so fine, so devastatingly painful in the whole world.

The fact remained that though I had resisted it, I had loved Charlene deeply and her loss was like my own twin had been pulled from my bones. Like a sickly child I stared with utter contempt at the plates of tea biscuits and digestives and fruitcake that the rector's wife would bring to me. No matter how many of these sweets I ate, I knew I could never be the devoted adopted son who was happy to loiter about the house and visit with members of the congregation. I could never sip tea with old ladies and talk in polite whispers. I could never share in the subtle joy of mince tarts and Spode china and Constable place-mats and Earl Grey tea or sit in conference with the rector Hugh Davis and comfortably list all the reasons that I had for appreciating the support and love and kindness that he had shown me.

When my month of sorrow had finished I came down from my room and I was polite with Bee, but I called the high school and asked them to mail my diploma to me. I then set about burying everything that Charlene had ever given me in a solemn ceremony by the rubble pile out back. I did not go to my graduation. I did not go to church any more with the rector's wife. I simply packed up the belongings of my little stale-smelling corner room and decided once and for all that I was leaving this place. On my way out the door, the rector's wife handed me my old Nestlé chocolates paper-route tin which housed one thousand dollars in rolled quarters, red two-dollar-bills and fives. "This money is for you, Selwyn," she said, "but you mustn't spend a penny of it until after you've been evaluated."

"I've already been evaluated," I whined. "By policemen. Fire chiefs. You and every self-righteous sod in the parish."

"Don't talk sharply with me, Selwyn. You haven't been evaluated by Dr. Günter."

"Who's Dr. Günter?"

"A leading child psychiatrist, Selwyn."

Chapter 17

Dr. Günter got up from his chair and flicked the light on in the room.

"There you have it, Dr. Günter." I uncrossed my legs and put my hands down over my knees. My head hurt. I was drunkish.

Dr. Günter contemplated the phone for a second. He pulled a sheet of paper from the middle drawer of his desk and began scratching on it.

"Do you have family in Vancouver, Selwyn?" he asked.

"No," I replied.

"Then why there?"

"Why not?"

"For the simple reason that you don't have family there."

"I don't have family here, Dr. Günter. My adopted father is dead. Bee is more of a schoolmarm than a mother. And the fire department in every county in the province of Nova Scotia is out to get me." I was irritated. "So what's the prognosis, doctor?"

I stretched like a cat, got up. Folded everything neatly.

"Does this mean I'm not going to jail?"

"Are you confessing to committing arson at the Lockhart residence?"

"I am not."

Dr. Günter rose, gathered his things. "There is no criminal evidence to apply against you. A feeling I have will not hold up well in a court of law."

"Then why have I been brought here?"

"Because what I do have is a say in whether you should be further evaluated."

"So I am not free to go?"

"My recommendation is that you see someone who will, through me, remain in contact with Bee." Dr. Günter placed his hands together, fingertips touching. "Selwyn. Why Vancouver?"

I felt rushed. I struggled with my coat. "Because it is as far away from here as I can get." I knew this was bad but how could I explain to this man that if I was to sink into the glorious mire of self-pity, I must have a ruse to keep these annoying people who seemed to need to care about me at bay. And so in a burst of panic, while sitting on the toilet, I had decided Vancouver, because it looked so wonderfully cold and tranquil, like a watery tomb.

Dr. Günter lowered his head and handed me a card. It read:

DR. PHILIP GARDENER
Psychiatrist and Psychoanalyst
Suite 1403
1282 West Broadway Medical Centre
Vancouver B.C.

"Dr. Gardener is a fine psychiatrist. He's a patient man and an old family friend. Odds are he will find your cynicism more charming than me and though I won't promise you anything, he is a good man and has been known to take in strays."

I fastidiously arranged all of my possessions and pocketed them. The old man stood and I noticed that he was more frail than I had imagined. He seemed just like the old rector to me and I was drawn to him. His voice was strong and arresting.

"Might I enquire where you are headed now, Selwyn?"

I turned towards him. Tipped my cap. "The diocesan centre," I said, "after that, the bus stop."

Bee fussed with me as we left the Halifax diocesan centre. "Come here," she said. I saw the hand go into the purse, the tissue come out. She licked the tissue, scrubbed my cheek.

"Is it enough to keep you going, dear?"

I looked at the cheque she had given me. Three hundred British pounds with the address of a British bank in Vancouver. It could have been worse. It could have been Canadian money. I felt guilty.

"You already gave me the paper-route tin, Bee. There is almost a thousand dollars in there."

"There's also money in Hugh's settlement if you want," she said. "For emergencies."

"I don't want the Rector's money," I replied.

"Is there anything good to come of this, of leaving, Selwyn?"

"Yes. You'll be relieved of the burden of worrying about me."

"A mother is never relieved of that burden, Selwyn."

"You're not my mother," I said.

"Hugh and I have raised you, Selwyn. That does count for something." A pause. "I expect that you will be back, Selwyn. There's always a place for you."

"I'm not coming back, Bee."

When the bus arrived, I went right onto the thing and sat in the first seat that I could find that was nowhere near any children or anyone who had an anxious look about them who might try to coax me into conversation. For a very long time I was happy in the nothingness of the driving, content in moving forwards as the bus droned along. I was only there as a face in the window, gaping at the beauty of the dark and hazy bog land, the flat red marshes, the little iron bridges with bulrushes underneath and dark tannin rivers that flowed beneath them. For a long time I stared at all this as if I was all alone in a chair in a great dark movie theatre. Very soon the monotony and the drone of the bus got the better of me. I was falling to sleep thinking of Charlene, my beautiful vulnerable Charlene, as I kissed her and picked the pillow feathers from her raven black hair.

Chapter 18
The Big Smoke

When I finally arrived in Toronto, I loitered in the bus station's public washroom because I couldn't stand the speed of the world outside me. The gunning of the taxi-cabs, the smog and pollution, the summer humidity, the smell of the streets, they were all such a shock that when I did muster the courage to bolt out into the world, I stood like a soldier on the street corner with my bags at my feet. After some time dodging taxis, I scurried into Chinatown, with a pack of beastly dogs trailing me. It was all such a scare, the clamour and roar of the place; I felt as if a giant plane was roaring over my head. I was so annoyed that I sent that rabble of dogs packing with a good stiff kick. Then I scuttled like a crab across the street, sought refuge under a fruit canopy and ferreted through fruit stalls for something to eat. I huddled there for some time mangling an orange, and after making harried enquiries about where I might stay for the night, I settled into a small hotel for which I paid far too much. In a state of grim and measured silence I hauled my things up the creaky stairs and sat like a spectre in the window, staring down morosely at the streets below.

Nursing a cheap bottle of Cold Duck, I sat drunk and gloomy, then stalked across the room and poked an odd-looking box in the corner which I took to be a television. I became very drunk as I sat there in front of that thing, fixated by the scenes of beauty and lust on the fashion station, the anorexic models, the flashbulbs, the celebrities in the front row. As I sat there in a wondrous stare of transfixion I filled with longing and regret for all the awful things I had done to Charlene's home. I wanted in my desperate way to pick up the phone and call poor old Bee and tell her that I loved her dearly. But I also knew that I couldn't call her in the state I was in.

When things started to blur I stumbled outside, where I scooped some ice into a bucket. I bent down and eyed a magazine in the garbage by the ice machine. The cover of the magazine showed a young Chinese girl with blue eyeliner wearing a tight halter top. She was holding a child. I knew as I stared at her and felt a certain buzz in my bits and pieces that I was now missing my darling Charlene something fierce. I lay on the bed and stared at the child and the woman and the curve of her stomach, where I imagined the child liked to sleep. I felt so suddenly homesick looking at them all. I went straight for the back of the book.

"Hello this is room 113. Do you have a *City* magazine?"

"What?"

"*City* magazine. I want someone who looks like the woman on the front."

"We have young Chineez modrel. Four hundred dollars. Fucky. No fucky. Same price."

"Send her."

The line went dead.

Su Chin, a pretty Taiwanese girl with blue eyes, arrived at my door.

"You do this lot?" she asked, sitting on the edge of my bed, pressing into the edges of the bed with her fingernails.

"Never before in my life." I passed her a glass of the sickly-sweet wine.

"You feel sad something?" she asked sharply.

"I feel like I've lost something," I replied. "I feel like I was given a package and lost it before I opened it."

"Unlucky," Su Chin replied, "very unlucky." She frowned. She took my hand. Flipped it over.

"Do you believe in ghosts, Mr. Selwyn?"

"I believe in ghouls and I was trailed by packs of them in high school."

Su Chin pouted slightly.

"My father say I'm haunted. He say skin like ghost. Head like horse. He say he never know me."

Su Chin looked at me strangely. I took another drink. Gave some to her. I lifted her blouse.

"Hands cold." She shivered.

I pulled off my shirt. Stepped out of my trousers.

"Go on," I said.

She dropped her skirt to the floor. Thumbs through white panties. Side to side. Down they went.

I stared at her womanhood. She looked just like Charlene down there. Black wool. Just less of it.

In the middle of the night I woke up.

"I feel like I need to confess something," I whispered in the light.

"What you want confess?"

"That I'm a coward," I said. "That I'm a pyromaniac and that I'm damned homesick and I miss an old woman who was married to a rector in a church in Nova Scotia."

"The lector's wife?"

"Her too," I said.

"Smells musty in here," Su Chin whispered. "Smells like sex," she said.

The next day I got up early and mailed a postcard back to the rector's wife. On it I wrote:

Oh the Lord is good to me
And so I thank the Lord
For giving me the things I need
The sun and the rain
and the apple seed
The Lord is good to me

I sang the song once. Then I started to cry.

CHAPTER 19

I was loathsome to myself as I bought my ticket at the Greyhound station in Toronto, partly because it was purchased with money that I had stolen back from Su Chin. I realized that I was hungover and sore and that I had no individual thought, desire or human feeling; I was just like some rusted bolt dragging slowly across the Canadian Shield, the Prairies, the Rocky Mountains, towards a half-working neon electromagnet called Vancouver.

Driving along in that rattling old bus, I was picking up bits of all the dark stinking residue of this strange country, the roadkill, the tire marks on the highways, duff, burned-out trees, dead mosquitoes, broken beer bottles, skunk scent and traplines. I imagined the bus a giant hunk of painted steel being pulled along and I started to entertain myself by making the little buzz-zapp sounds that I imagined giant wrecking-yard electromagnets made. I must have irritated the whole bus, because when we stopped for breakfast no one would talk to me, and I sat alone at the table in the Revelstoke Mohawk station staring at the great fir trees outside and picking at my eggs and bacon. A Native woman with a rugrat child asked me if I wanted to go splits on a case of Pepsi but I took one look at that snotty faced little bugger and turned the funny faces in my egg yolk into sad ones.

Chapter 20
Vancouver

When I got to Vancouver I walked right through the bus terminal with the address in my hand, the address of Dr. Philip Gardener. I sat quietly in the public transit as it drove slowly over the bridge and towards Broadway. While I sat there, trying to keep the uncertainty I felt at bay, I stared at the mountains, at the billowing sky and at the dark building cranes that looked like insects stalking through the murky blue/black harbour. I thought many horrible things and imagined that the man I was going to see had cancelled all his appointments for that morning and was sitting in his room saving up his all his rage for a ten-minute blast at me.

When I eventually found the psychiatrist's building, a fifteen-storey affair with cathedral-like spires bathed in cold grey light, I stood in the doorway and obsessed about this meeting. The more I stood in that doorway, the more nervous and fearful I felt. Still I pressed on, past the security officer and his bored stare, till I was in the elevator pushing the doors closed, jabbing my fingers at the buttons. I looked at myself in the mirror, staring at my drawn and vaguely handsome teenage face, and hating myself for what I felt I ought to do rather than what I wanted to do. Still I was going up, watching the round red floor lights flashing. Three. Four. Five. Holding in my hand the card which read:

Dr. Philip Gardener
Psychiatrist and Psychoanalyst
Suite 1403
1282 West Broadway Medical Centre
Vancouver B.C.

When the elevator reached the twelfth floor an earnest woman stepped on, holding her purse at her chest. She took the card from my hand and gave me a quick maternal glance. "You're on the wrong floor. The fourteenth floor is two flights up, young man."

The resoluteness of her tone, the utter certainty of what she said, the way she evaluated me as if everything bad in life were a mere hand scratch and a pill prescription away from being cured, made me flush with anger. And so in that bleak but elating moment, I took that woman by the hand. I told her that therapists and psychiatrists were for the weak, and that it was the weak and lonely who went like sheep to them. I saw in her eyes that she could see that I was just an eighteen-year-old scared wretch with a runny nose and an ass that burned from sitting on it for three days. Suddenly I felt the falseness of what I had said. I hugged the woman like a tree, then I shot like a firecracker down the steps and out the door. Away from the doctor at the end of the corridor with the white coat and the wispy crown of thinning hair and that somnolent gaze I knew all too well.

I walked for what seemed like hours across the bridge, back towards the old bus station because it was a reference point, and then past the bus station till I came upon the Derry Hotel, just off East Hastings. There was something comforting about the place, the fading red neon sign above which was misspelled HOTL, the wobbly vermiculite tables with food crusted in the joins, the grease stench and the short waitress who fried my breakfast on a rusted brown heating-pad behind the counter. When the old girl finished serving me she sat near the window with an old man who drank coffee and coughed and had a silvery stubble on his chin. I stared at the man in the sunlight. His face was caved in and sunken and his cheekbones looked burnished like a new shoe; his head nodded up and down as if in time to a song.

As I sat there, I began to think that the old man was roughly the same age as the rector would have been had he lived a few more years. And the woman, as ugly as she was, had some of the practicality of Bee in her. There was a trace of the familiar in her, albeit a sad and desolate familiarity, as if she had once been legendary for a salty brand of humour but the raucous laugh which accompanied it now sounded more lonely than cruel. I sat there and fretted and tried desperately not to look at people who came in the door. I began to think about Charlene and about her mother packing the lot of them into the car in the middle of the night. I thought of baby Hector strapped into the back seat or cradled in Charlene's arms, Marlene telling them all to be quiet as she drove down the little pot-holed rural road, through the fields of cow corn and towards the main highway that led to the road south to the United States. Soon I was sucking on the dregs of my coffee, nose running, eyes cold and on fire. I was just cursing when I paid the bill. I gave the old creature ten bucks, didn't wait for the change and started walking down the streets. Past plastic neon coffee shops, past shoe shops, record stores, store windows with mannequins swathed in beautiful silks. I stood at the base of a church near the corner of East Hastings and Cambie and huddled with my arms wrapped around my knees in the wet drizzle and rain. My vision blurred in the mist. I rubbed at my eyes and saw to my horror shadows rushing here and there, then between my legs a tail, a rat's tail. I stamped at it hysterically and looked up, alarmed.

There in front of me I saw a woman with a face so thin, so long and lost that I waved my hand towards her instinctively. She was in sweatpants and her arms were crossed over her chest, little nipples like pencil points through her shirt. She was coming towards me, walking and tripping and saying in a voice that was quiet and whispery but loud enough so that I could hear nothing else, "Hey you. Don't I know you boy, don't I know you boy?" And I looked into her face, her skin white with little red blemishes on her chin. Her eyes were as small and dark as ink spots. I looked at her mouth, which drew thinner and thinner, pulling away from her teeth, and then it was the shine of a cheap tiny stud earring. I saw a man behind her, wearing a faded Expos cap. The man grinned at me. In an instant day became night.

CHAPTER 21

I awoke with my shirt in the bushes and my pockets pulled out and a sudden longing for that Chinese girl I had had back at that hotel in Toronto. My eyes were sore and my mouth hummed like I had been stung by bees. When I got past the ache in my mouth and my knee I held my head. In front of me I saw a form and the gleam of a belt buckle, whitish silver, which hurt my eyes. I squinted at the floral pattern on it:

1967
Pincher Creek Rodeo
Boys Steer Wrestling Champ

Beyond the buckle were brass rivets, stitching, wiry legs jammed through indigo Wranglers, an orange cowboy shirt buttoned at the neck and a rugged boy's face crested with shocks of dirty blond hair. The mouth on that face was grinning like it had just shoved itself full of dog shit from the pavement. Standing beside the cowboy was another desperate-looking soul with long thinning blond hair and shiny green sunglasses that gave him the appearance of a gecko. When I saw the creature with the sunglasses splash some vodka onto the red gash at my knee I kicked at him.

"Hurts, don't it?" said Mr. Sunglasses, stooping over me.

Mr. Sunglasses and the handsome one, Clark, took me down a back street that smelled of exhaust and gasoline. I was wearing a hood that the cowboy had given me and I was shivering more from shock than from cold. The cowboy didn't say much, but he had a gentleness and a kindness about him that I liked. When we got going I noticed that he had a tattoo of a running horse down his arm. He had a rugged, physical beauty about him, the kind of beauty I'd seen in the ads of cowboys smoking cigarettes that Bee had saved as a girl and shown me when I was a child. I was intrigued because the cowboy seemed to be unaware of his good looks, and had a shy way about him and said "yup" lots and "sure" and "thet be good." I heard the sound of his boots on the pavement as we walked along. For a long time I avoided eye contact with the other one because I could sense in him a need to talk. In a strange way, though I didn't know either of these two from Adam, I felt safe being with them. When we rested beside a dumpster Mr. Sunglasses spat at the pavement, near my foot.

"Queerin' round Clean Rigs park, eh..."

For the first time I got a good hard look at Mr. Sunglasses, whose face behind the glasses was more youthful than I might have imagined.

"Lost," I said, "Mr. Sunglasses."

"I'm Carl," he grunted.

"I'm adopted," I said.

"Runaway, eh?"

I didn't answer. I felt cold all of a sudden. I could feel a wetness behind my ear. The cowboy pulled his bandana from around his neck and wiped me with it. I took it from him and stared at the black cruddy blood there. I looked back at Mr. Sunglasses. He was taking a draw on a bottle of vodka. In his sunglasses I read:

Chapter 22

I passed out on a couch in the Sunspot Lounge, where the cowboy and Mr. Sunglasses and their band, the ills, were performing. Sometime during the evening I was dragged into the bathroom and washed by two strong girls who had some dealing with the band. The one with the skirt and dark hair had a kind way about her and laid me down and whispered "that's okay" in my ear as I looked at the fluorescent lights above and counted the colours and blotches in my eyes.

Then she squeezed my hand and I heard the sink run. I saw her step over me and smile a bit and when I knew what she was doing, washing me and cleaning me, I told her that I wanted her to teach me how to do it like that and she laughed and was out the door with a shy glance round for good measure. I liked that look so much that I yelled after her that I liked that look even more than what she had done to me. Then I was led down the corridor past the packed gear and dark instrument cases by a competent and determined redhead named Jules. But before I could get out another clever word or thank her for her kindness, I collapsed into the back of the band van, like a fist.

When I awoke the next morning I was cold, staring at a pile of hockey decals pressed into the top of the van. I had a hard-on that hurt like hell. It hurt more when I thought of what that goddamned woman in the bathroom had done with a small hand no bigger than a baseball. Clark and Mr. Sunglasses came into the van and sat beside me. They smelled like gasoline or some kind of stinky glue and they were both on me like animals, rubbing me harshly up down up down on the arms and putting stinky fingers in my face and saying stinky pinky real loud. Before they were done my chest and legs were bruised from fighting them and trying to defend myself. Clark seemed to have the most sense of the pair. He would compulsively roll duct tape into a ball in his hand. I trusted Clark a little more than Mr. Sunglasses because his line of questioning, in between gleeful yelps and duct-tape rolling, revolved around what the hell I knew about amps and electrical cords and carpentry for shit's sake.

Both of them stared at me like I was their own prize find. Clark was going "since it seems that you have no life at all I feel pleased to tell you we need a roadie 'cause the Chief Willie Kinson was a shit for brains who formed his own band and the guy before that we left on the side of the road in Vernon 'cause he was always trying to screw the sound girl from Montreal who was sleeping under the bunk with that long-haired loudmouth promoter from Toronto." Mr Sunglasses was grinning, peering over his glasses and going, "Runaway, eh?" He poked me in the ribs with his one-hitter, packed tight with good Vancouver weed. Soon we were all sitting in the sun of the parking lot. They needled me and plied me with drink and smoke and I lay in the sun and listened to them talk. A terrible inertia crept over me and I knew as I drank and listened to their stories and careless tales that if I did not go now I would never escape.

Very soon I was drunk and giddy and full of shame for having gotten in with them so easily. But I was also alive with the feeling of it all being alright for once, and I began boasting with them as well. I soon felt at ease with the cowboy. He told me all the crummy names for cock and balls in a non-stop ten-minute diatribe while he walked along in his boots and compacted duct tape in his hand incessantly. Soon enough we were walking tall and wildly down the streets of East Hastings near the Sunspot Lounge, where the boys had played the night before. When we got in I started to feel some sense of happiness again and I ordered food from the waitress with money that I bummed from Clark, who seemed to have scads of it on him. Before I got into it with Clark, or started tearing into a rant about all the fun and silliness of being well-fed again, Mr. Sunglasses was beside me giving me shit about how you're not supposed to order food and eat it when you are supposed to be drinking.

Jules, the redhead, watched me for a long uncomfortable

time at the bar while I ignored Mr. Sunglasses and shovelled food into my gullet. When I was done she lit a smoke and eyed me shrewdly.

"So," she said, "everybody in this bar has something they're good at. I'm a witch. Clark's a cowboy. Carl's a hopeless drunk and that"—she pointed to a quiet man sitting at the bar holding an Adidas bag with two tiny ferrets peeking out of it—"is my old man, Jeff Rook. He sings for the band. What is it that you do?"

"Imitate rabbits," I said. I steadied myself. Relaxed my throat muscles.

"Do what?" she asked.

"This," I said. Hands outstretched.

The cigarette dropped from her mouth like a log. Faces at the bar swivelled a perfect 90 degrees.

The next morning I awoke at the back of a hurtling cube van that was attempting an ascent up a mountain pass. I looked out the front window at the trees rushing past, the sunlight reflecting off the tops of the pale mountains and the tiny slit of emerald at the bottom. I was hungover but I shouted through the doors at the driver.

"Where are we going?" I asked.

"Next gig." Was the answer.

"Next gig where?"

"Banff."

Clark pulled the curtains away from his bunk. "Wanna job?" he asked tiredly, taking a swig from a half-empty bottle of orange Crush.

"Doin' what?"

"Doin' whatever. Haulin' gear, sellin' merchandise. Roadie shit."

"How much?"

"Ten bucks per diem. All the fries you can eat." Clark snapped an eye patch back over his eyes and leaned back in his bed.

"That's slave wages."

"Free room and board," he murmured from beneath the layers.

I grabbed the stinking cushions. "These cushions are filthy, they're covered in chocolate stains and there's ketchup from somebody's fries."

"Nose bleeds," said the guitarist, Jesse, a hulking form with fiery red sideburns. He sat upright in the bunk above, then peered down at me, gloating. "And that isn't chocolate. Those are shit stains."

Chapter 23
Roadie

I remained with the band a month, a year and then three years because the simple truth of the matter was that I had nowhere else to go. I soon got used to the rigours of hauling amplifiers, guitars, drum kits, bass pedals and merchandise up and down stairs and in and out of cheap hotels and seedy bars and dance clubs and pubs. I soon became oblivious to the poor pay, the nights of interrupted sleep and the continuous drone of the cube van hurtling somewhere between Moosonee and Grande Prairie. I relished the anonymity of this life, the fact that I had to do little, think little and only exist in the day in, day out mild drudgery of an unsuccessful touring rock band. At eighteen, nineteen, twenty, I could feel my body running on but I felt perfectly content in having no responsibilities to anyone but myself.

As the years passed, I became the back-door Annie of the band, always around to help load and unload gear. I learned to mask my hypersensitivity and tantrums because no one would listen to me. When I really needed to talk about some horrible, terrorizing fear, I cornered Clark. Though he said little, when he did talk he spoke to me like he didn't know what anything meant either. I felt a definite and sure-fire ease with him. I also felt in awe of him, as if in our own reckless forwards thrust, we were opposite halves of the same flawed, sad, beautiful and ugly human being. I hit the bottle more than I ever had, and learned that my drinking in high school was kids' play. I learned that when I bragged about my time with the prostitute I was full of shit. I learned that wine and syrupy cocktails were pussy drinks and that vodka and rye were what real men had.

As the years passed, the pain I felt about Hector and Charlene and the guilt I felt about not contacting the rector's wife just became part of the blurred and booze-soaked haze that was my complicated past. For the first time in my life, I felt a deadening affirmation that this was my fate, and that there was some degree of luck in this fate—to have fallen in with this band of misfits who paid me next to nothing, yet never required that I give up a damned thing of myself.

Three years became five years. I learned how to play guitar, how to imitate the band's songs in the back of the van. I learned how to seduce girls and how to pretend that I was less interested in what I was doing than I really was. Most importantly, I learned how to release the rabbit screech at will when one of those boorish misfits got too close to me. Everything was rolling along in a nice, quiet, comforting drone till one Tuesday in May, four years after I joined the band:

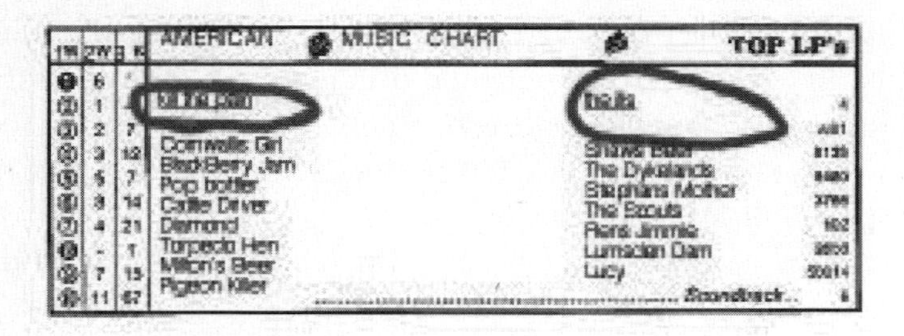

Chapter 24

Everything changed. The band's fringe audience of drop-outs, deadbeats, drug addicts and disenfranchised kids multiplied tenfold when their one and only hit, "Kill the Pain," first picked up by KROQ in North L.A., went to number five on the Billboard alternative-rock charts. Suddenly this little-known Edmontonian fringe band was all the rage. The song "Kill the Pain"—a shit stain of a song stuck on their sixth album at the last minute because of a lag in continuity between side A and side B—became the single most requested rock song of that year. You couldn't turn on The Music Station without seeing Clark standing with his legs splayed, sticking his tongue out and picking at his bass. You couldn't turn on the radio without hearing Jeff Rook crying into the microphone:

You've got to Ki - i - il the pain,
You've got to nil the shame
You've got to know its name
and all
and all
and all
that matters

The damned song became so popular that the band was asked to perform it at civic holidays and Canada Day celebrations and Klondike Days in its hometown of Edmonton. In fact, the success nearly did the boys in. That year the ills were asked to become ambassadors for Alberta Tourism; they were asked to smile in their promotional stills instead of glowering disdainfully as was their inclination.

Almost as soon as the money came, rifts developed within the band. Clark began to hint at a desire to form a splinter grass-roots country/western band and Jeff, the lead singer, and Mr. Sunglasses were threatening to form their own death-metal band. The tension in the cube van was unbearable. Hours would go by without any of the band members speaking and everyone would spray out of the van at the next small town to play video games or bike the lonely streets or comb bookstores. At night every anxiety and disappointment and uncommunicated hate would be reflected in a hard-slamming performance of that damned three-minute pop song all three thousand kids had come out for—"Kill the Pain."

I decided to pack it all in in Edmonton when the band returned home after three years of continuously touring. The simple truth was that though I had been accepted into this life, I had grown to despise the infighting, the constant sizing up from other gruesome roadies who were in less successful bands, the bickering between band and promoter—and especially the endless and moronic drone of "Kill the Pain." While I had grown close to members of the band, especially Clark, I had also grown to loathe the conforming that happens amongst groups of people, the endless standing around and waiting for someone to suggest what crummy restaurant to eat in. The constant lazy *fer sures* and *no doubts* and *she's pipin' 'er eh* which preceded every sentence. But each time I tried to tell the band that I wanted to leave, I couldn't spit out the words for I had no friends to speak of in this world besides that goddamned stud in spurs, that broom stick with sunglasses, that hulking leprechaun guitarist and Jeff, the lead singer with the ferrets. While I was obsessing over how to tell them that my eight years of servitude were up, I was dismayed to find that I didn't have the resolve and strength of character to just tell them. My awkwardness around the band was starting to grate hard on Clark's and Mr. Sunglasses' nerves. I was sure they were going to fire me. However, before they left me standing with my bags packed on the side of the road to Fort Saskatchewan, their eccentric lead singer provided me with an unusual but timely exit.

Standing at the front of the stage one night in Edmonton doing an encore during the Kill The Pain Again Tour, Jeff froze, staggered and then dropped like a stone into a sea of weeping teens. When he failed to resurface, Jesse dropped into the mosh pit to bring him back. Cradled in Jesse's arms, Jeff didn't utter a sound but his eyes remained open.

"Part of the act," said the kids.

"It's the drugs," said the journalists covering the show.

But when Jeff's jaw locked the next day, he was rushed to hospital and a doctor found a puncture wound on his elbow that looked suspiciously like the teeth markings of a pet ferret. When one of the ferrets was found dangling from a chair with its teeth embedded in the wood, an autopsy revealed a rabid vole inside the dead ferret's stomach lining.

The next day the *Edmonton Star* ran this headline:

LOCK JAW SILENCES RAW NERVE

As the cards and well-wishes flooded in, there amongst the cards and envelopes I spotted a dainty but dog-eared letter postmarked:

THE RECTORY
FOX HILLS RD.
KINGS COUNTY
NOVA SCOTIA

I fought with the wrapper.

Silly Child,

I have resisted contacting you these last years as I am something of an optimist at heart and I have always felt that good comes of the bad in the end. Hugh would have said that the decisions that a young man makes in his life must be his own. I want you to know that I have waited in this old house for nearly eight years and I have thought of you as any mother would.

I want you to know that your absence and your

> silence trouble me. I think you should know that my health, in the last few years, has deteriorated. My joints are swelling, I need help getting in and out of the bath, I have food delivered for me twice weekly and I have to pay a gardener to keep the place looking sharp. I'm not asking you to come back home and look after me, dear boy, as I know that would be the worst decision for all involved, but I do think a courtesy call is the absolute minimum that I can expect from you, even if it is me who must pay. (I don't say that to be rude, but rather expect that it is the case.) Do be a dear and call at a reasonable time as I'll be in bed after ten.
>
> Yours very dearly,
> Mother
> (Bee)
>
> P.S. I have put some of Hugh's money away for you and the stock does seem to have done rather well.

I capitalized on the vulnerability of the ills, all of us hovering around Jesse's bed.

"Clark," I whispered in the hospital room, "I need my roadie pay."

"Fer what?" he asked, looking down at poor paralyzed Jeff.

"Plane fare," I answered. "My adopted mother's going senile on me."

I looked at Jeff, whose mouth had formed a perfect "O".

Clark looked at me. "Adopted mother? I never knew ya were adopted."

"You never asked," I said.

"When you coming back?"

I paused for a second. The time seemed right. "I'm not," I said.

Chapter 25

So all the way back home. Cab fare to airport. $85.00. Flight Edmonton to Toronto. $285. Flight Toronto to Halifax. $199.00. I huddled on the side of the Sackville highway in a warm band sleeping bag and hitchhiked down the 101 for free. When I arrived, the rector's wife was on the lawn in the back of the house, sitting in a wheelchair with an afghan across her lap. She was stretching to pick berries from a poorly pruned dwarf sour-cherry tree.

"Selwyn, dear," she chuckled. And I, standing underneath a pair of pink undergarments on the clothesline, dropped everything I was carrying to my feet.

"Yes," I said meekly, "it's me."

That evening I became a ten-year-old boy once again. I warmed her teapot, placed two P.G. Tips packets in the pot, placed the tea cozy over the top and walked stiff-backed into the living-room with a plate of Marks-and-Sparks chocolate digestives and the full Spode tea set.

"It's so nice to have you home, dear."

"It won't be for long..." I said tensely, looking up from the little globs of sour cream that were floating in my tea.

"Well," she began brightly the next morning, "I've planned a trip for us to make as I don't know how long it is that you intend to stay. Really Selwyn, this is a beautiful part of the world and I do think we should take advantage of the bright weather and see some of it."

"I hate trips," I replied. "I've been hurtling across the prairies in the back of a garbage truck for eight years."

The rector's wife ignored me. "I'm going to pack a picnic lunch and the both of us will spend the day at Terence Bay. It'll be just like when you were a child. Don't you think it'll be delightful, Selwyn?"

"Delightful is not the word that comes to mind, Bee," I replied.

By the time we got to Terence Bay it was fogged in. I cut a swath down through the wild roses and the Queen Anne's lace and the brambles towards the rocks where I lay on a large flat stone. I helped the rector's wife down the muddy slope and we sat there. For a long time we stared at the black shiny Bay of Fundy with the scent of seaweed and sewage and decaying fish and cool salt thick in the air. We ate our sandwiches and the rector's wife pulled her blanket across her legs.

"I just wish you happiness, Selwyn. When you were young you were such a marvellous musician, Selwyn."

"I should have kept with it," I said, etching some retribution onto a stone, "but I cocked it up like I cocked up Charlene."

"There's no need to talk so rudely, Selwyn. What would Hugh think if he heard you talking like that?"

"He wouldn't like it, Bee. But I'm too old to care what he thinks now."

The rector's wife paused for a few moments, then pulled an orange from out of the hamper and tried to peel it. "Selwyn, dear."

Hearing the word "dear," I knew something was up.

"Would it bother you if I tried to help you find your true parents?"

"Bother me? I'm not interested in knowing about some pair of cowards. How would you feel if someone did the same to you?"

The rector's wife drew silent.

"Selwyn, must you be so naughty?" I felt so distraught that I closed my eyes and began, in a soft voice, a little disconsolate hum. I held her hand.

"I'm sorry Bee. I don't feel entirely comfortable in this world sometimes. It's not your fault."

Old-lady tears. The worst kind. "Selwyn, why must you be such a worry?"

"I loved Charlene, Bee. She has my child. I felt like I finally had something apart from you and Hugh that I could call my own and it was taken from me."

"If we'd had some patience. It all could have been sorted out." A wipe.

"I am glad to see you, Bee. Really." I said.

"And me you, you silly dear."

I felt happy to be there with her. We both closed our eyes.

When I opened them she was silently making her way up the dirty embankment with one hand on her knee. I gathered up all the perishables from the picnic table, placed them back in the picnic hamper and followed her up towards the car.

Chapter 26

That night I said good night coolly to the rector's wife and kissed her as was the custom, then I went briskly to my old bedroom, lay down on top of the eiderdown and stared at the ceiling of the bedroom that had been mine since I was a small boy. I looked at the yellowing ceiling tiles above. Much about the house had not changed, the sound of a tractor grinding its way up a back road behind the rectory, the clank and hum of farmyard machinery, the yells and calls of farm-hands, the whispers of crickets and ciccadas and the startled outrage of a spooked pheasant, flying through the trees.

Here I was back home, the place where I felt as if I was three inches tall. Here I was in this old place where the smell of manure over fields made my eyes water, where flies as big as bumblebees ruined afternoon picnics. Here I was in this town where I had murdered pigeons with Jerry O'Reardon and stepped on live frogs and walked out on the dyke fields and found kittens in plastic ice-cream containers, bugs and worms crawling out of eye sockets. Here I was in this town where I had seen my own pet rabbit, the lovely and winsome Amanda, raped by Winchester—and I had done nothing but stare in intrigue and wonder and fascination at the gruesome act.

Chapter 27

The phone rang in the middle of the night but I was so exhausted I didn't hear it. I stared at the rector's wife standing in the doorway, the dim light tracing the contours of her dowdy frame. She held the door handle as if to steady herself. "Selwyn, dear," she said, her voice dry, "there's a young gentleman on the phone for you."

I rolled off the bed, stumbled across the grey linoleum floors and mumbled a thank you as I pulled the receiver to my ear.

"Hullo."

"Selwyn Davis. Hah, hah." The voice was a half-squawk.

"Clark."

I pulled the receiver closer to my mouth. His voice was rushed.

"We're goin' back on tour. Comin' er what?"

"How's Jeff? Is he better?"

"He's in hospital."

"I know he's in hospital."

"Psychiatric hospital. They say he's got brain poisoning."

"God. What are his chances of recovery?"

"Zero to none."

Tension.

"Is the tour still on?"

"Yeah. We booked more dates..."

"How can you tour with no lead singer?"

"Had a vote."

"Vote?" I pronounced the word dumbly like Clark had.

"We've been auditioning fer about two weeks. But most of the guys were pretty much pipin' 'er. "

"Pipin' 'er..." The open-vowelled tone of Clark's words now seemed distasteful and alien to me. I'd forgotten that Clark was so straightforward, so matter-of-fact. Dare I say he sounded dumb?

"A lot a those guys who auditioned were trying to sound like Axyl er whatever. Pipin' 'er."

"So who's singing?"

"Me and the boys want you to sing."

"Me? But I can't sing?"

"You can screech like a rabbit and that's pretty much the shape of 'er. The thing is the whole thing's gotta be true to your art and you, when you screech the rabbit screech, no one does that shit but you."

"You talked to the band about this?"

"Yep."

"Well," I was starting to awaken now, the nervousness coming back again. "They're just as crazy as you are. I'm not singing in some band I don't even know half the songs of. I'm not telling lies to fans about songs I didn't write. I'm not satisfying some sick fantasy of yours."

"Yer comin'. It's all settled."

"No I'm not." I glanced over my shoulder towards the rector's wife who, I was relieved to find had, left me in peace to talk. "I'm not singing and I'm not sleeping on that damned shit-and blood-soaked roadie bed ever again."

"Don't have to, we refurbished the tour bus with the last royalty check"

"It's still a coffin on wheels."

"You get Jeff's bunk. It's the best of them all."

"I'm not sleeping in some haunted demon bed. Not a damned chance." I went to hang up the phone, but I felt suddenly lonely. If I hung up the phone it would never ring again and I would be enslaved by the rector's wife, forced to can plums and tomatoes in summer and clear the driveway in the winter. If I hung up the phone now what were the chances that I would ever talk with Clark again or that I would have another normal friendship? I hesitated, tried to sound confident. "Call me when you get back, Clark. Maybe you can do a mall signing through the Annapolis Valley."

"We just got signed on to tour with the Hellions, Selwyn. We're touring France and Germany and then Thailand and Japan."

"Well," I stammered, "I'm scared of planes and I hate hot weather."

"I just want you to come on tour with us. It'd be fun, Selwyn."

"It's a goddamned nightmare is what it is..." But something in Clark's voice had become familiar. It reeked of care and hope and concern and joy and all things that made me love, yes love, this dopey cowboy.

"What else you gonna do, Selwyn?"

"Well I thought I might write my own thoughts about things. There's a lot I want to get down on paper."

"Write it on the road. Maybe we can play a few of your songs."

I stiffened. "There's the simple matter of payment. I can't live on roadie pay."

"Per diem's doubled and a hundred bucks a week."

"It's still goddamned slave wages."

"So stay home, then."

Just like that. My contact with anything good and hopeful and uplifting crumbled like cake. I looked at the receiver. I put the phone down. In the next room I could hear Bee buzzing away in slumber. That settled everything. I bought the ticket the next day.

Chapter 28

When I got up the next day the Bee insisted on driving me to the airport in the old rectory car. She wore a dark scarf and her hair was done and blue rinsed so that traces of the dye stained her housecoat. She wore lipstick, which I am loath to say made her look like a sad old clown.

"Selwyn," she said, "I want to be with you before you go. I just want to spend a few minutes with you in the car before you go. I can't think of anything more awful than dropping you off at the airport and seeing you off as if I don't give a damned care in the world about my son."

I stared out the window and bit on my lower lip and replied sullenly. "I do know that you care about me. I do know that, so you don't have to keep reminding me." I held her hand firmly. "I do know that you care about me, so you don't have to say it."

"Well," she cleared her throat, "I'm glad that you feel that way Selwyn. There's such a strain now. Everything seems such a strain..."

I looked at her and I realized she was scared. As much as I wanted to stay and take care of her, I knew that staying would solve nothing for either of us. Bee would manage without me. She still had many parish friends who came round to keep her company and we both knew she would be far happier in the long run with me gone and not moping around her house. Still, my heart broke to see her after all this time and I hoped she knew it better now. I stood there awkwardly and hugged her hard. "Bee," I said finally, just as stiff and firm as Hugh would have, "I do love you, you know."

Chapter 29
Clark Lied

Clark lied. The ills didn't start touring for another month, but he had been eager to get me out to Mother Alberta so that he could break me in to the rigours of playing sets with the band. And so I arrived in Edmonton, shuffling through the arrivals lounge with a quilt draped over my shoulders and sniffling because I'd caught a chill on the plane.

Clark threw the two hockey bags that contained everything I had to my name into the back of his great wide black 1968 Dodge Polaris. We drove the boat into the city and headed down White Avenue where we stopped to pick up some monitor heads and then drove straight to the band's garage.

I was not given a chance to even get a drink or sit down. Jerry, the fiery red-headed bassist who looked like a cross between Ronald McDonald and Satan, greeted me at the doorway: "Rock star er what?" he asked.

"No," I replied disdainfully, "hired hand."

Mr. Sunglasses beat his sticks down on the drum, "So. We playin er pipin' 'er?"

I looked around the garage, which housed a punching bag in the corner, a half-empty canister of gasoline, a lawnmower, some flaking patio furniture and three of the ugliest snotty-nosed children I had ever seen.

"What are these rugrats doing here?" I yelled, pointing at them.

"They're my niece's kids," responded Jerry, glowering. "You gotta problem with that?"

"No," I groaned.

And so I whispered and grunted and talked through the whole set, the kids just staring at me balefully and yawning till I got to the band's showstopper, "Kill the Pain," which I knew the words to and wrecked my throat trying to sing.

"Now yer gettin' 'er, Selwyn!" yelled Clark.

Chapter 30

From then on I seemed to be goaded into acting as peculiarly and offensively as possible, to speedily build a repertoire of idiosyncratic habits and sayings and tics that fit in with the anxiety, brutishness and carnival antics that were the hallmarks of the ills' sound. It was misery.

I couldn't for the life of me relax for the first while. I stared with fear at the mic and gyrated stiffly, shuffling my feet backwards and forwards, pressing my hands together in a prayer stance, trying to imitate Jeff. I knew it looked bad. I knew from the way that Mr. Sunglasses refused to look at me from behind the drum set, shaking his head from side to side. I knew from the way that Clark watched my feet, his tongue hanging out like a tired dog. I knew from the perpetual smirk on Jerry's face that I was making a damned fool of myself and that they knew that they had made a mistake in hiring me.

Halfway through another hopeless rendition of "Kill the Pain," the band stopped. I dropped the microphone to the floor.

"What????" I hissed.

"Well, I think you shouldn't try so hard er somethin'." Clark picked at his lip.

"Try so hard?"

Jerry looked at me. "He means the chit chat between songs."

"I'm just trying to get comfortable..." I protested, "I'm just trying to get into a rhythm."

"You're way too stiff..." Mr. Sunglasses got up from the drums, sat on a milk crate and took a swig from a forty of good ol' Alberta vodka. "Way too stiff er something'," he gulped.

"Well," I protested, "you brought me out here."

"Clark brought you out here," Mr. Sun Glasses took another swig, screwed the cap back on the bottle. "We had no goddamn say in it."

"Well I should just go, then..."

"The thing is," Clark put the bass down, "you got it in you, that's the thing, Selwyn. You're just not lettin' it out. You gotta sing like you talk. Mad."

"Pipin' 'er, pipin' 'er, pipin' 'er..." Mr. Sunglasses was yelling at no one. "Everybody's just pipin' 'er."

Jerry sat down glumly. Then he looked at me, looked right through me, and I knew he knew what a damned coward I really was for being there. Everything went silent and strange and I felt like I was being surrounded. Everyone was watching me and I was watching myself, sitting there with three strangers, a complete and utter poseur singing for them in their band.

Behind me I heard a door burst open and I felt a body come at me and felt arms wrap round me. I turned and got a look at my tormentor. It was Merle, Jesse's brother, and he was bear-hugging me from behind.

Jesse came forward, unbuckling his pants at his waist; he yanked them down to his knees and then stood there in his Mickey-Mouse boxer shorts.

"Ready to greet the cheesie?" he asked.

"Cheesie?"

He stretched his thumb under the elastic waistband and yanked 'em down. I closed my eyes at first, but I had to open them again; his skin was warm and smelled of musk. I peered at his little William, which was no bigger than a small snail, and with red moss billowing, it was thrust at me.

"Piss er touch?" he demanded.

"Yew! Yew! Yew!" Everybody, Clark, Mr. Sunglasses and Jesse, were yipping like braves dancing around a fire.

I was wrenching my head from side to side, everything imploding in my head at once. I clenched my teeth and saw images of fire and charred limbs and dead flies and rotting bloated skin and dust, gathering as if in a storm. I wrenched my hands free and pressed them to my ears. Everyone including Clark backed off as I threw out my hands and opened my mouth:

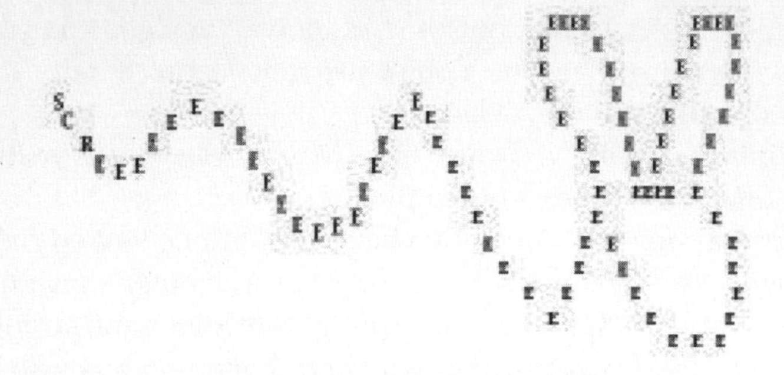

"My ears man, my ears!" Mr. Sunglasses was clutching the sides of his head and I saw Jesse in the doorway looking back at me, pissing into a white bucket that contained cigarette butts, beer caps and dead ants. Clark looked at me and then at Jerry. He nodded his head up and down. "Think you pretty much gotter, Selwyn," he said.

We played a few more sets, mainly in suburbs of Edmonton like Fort Saskatchewan and Leduc, places where the audiences were loyal to the hometown band, and didn't just favour the one hit song they'd heard on coffee breaks in their offices or on the am dial of their car radios driving home.

Performing in front of eight hundred devoted ills fans excited me. I sensed a genuine feeling of support from the fans, though deep inside I loathed having to talk with them after shows, and I loathed myself for having to sing someone else's songs. I started to get my legs, I suppose, in Leduc. I developed a singing pitch higher than Jeff's husky voice. It seemed that the unique squealing timbre of my voice, as well as the taunts I threw at the kids in the front row of the audience, endeared me to the band and, in an odd way, to the fans I ridiculed. I began to accumulate tics and habits, crazed head-back stares, an involuntary knee collapse. I began performing in clothes that I'd found at previous gigs and I encored each show with one of my trademark rabbit screams.

When we finally arrived in Vancouver to play one last set before our European tour with the all-female band the Hellions, I thought I was ready. I had nowhere else to go, no skills that could get me a job as a useful member of society and a serious fear of being shipped back to the parish of St. Peter's. I was not happy, but the one grain of hope in this was that I had a future as the lead singer of a rock band that had yet to write another album.

The last show we played in Vancouver was at the Sunspot Lounge, the same place I had met Clark all those years before. I sat after the show with Will, the drunk ex-roadie. In between flicking beer caps into my groin and taking long hungry draws on his Kokanee, he stopped dead serious and looked at me. Then he told me in a serious and scornful tone that I had no place on tour with this band and that I was nothing short of an impostor.

Chapter 31

Canada looked like one giant dirty over-flooded swamp from the plane. Just water and ice and dark trees and plots of earth and then sea. The clouds, wisps and mist and then clear blue sky, seemed as far away as the moon in summertime, and yet I felt drawn to their glorious whiteness, their softness, their peaceful contours. They seemed as dreamy to me as two days of sleep. The urge to open the plane window and fall out and tumble down and down into the seas was immeasurable. Jerry and Clark sat quietly side by side in the seats in front, trying on the headphones, politely asking for more buns and coffee and bags of peanuts, and reading through the entertainment section of the in-flight magazine, scouring it for a write-up of the band or any new press on "Kill the Pain." Mr. Sunglasses clearly wanted no part of this and was tense and sluggish, sipping tumbler after tumbler of vodka, yelling at us all to get liquored. I knew as each shot went into his head and as he reeled up and down the aisles looking like a worried old man that he was dreading the upcoming tour.

Chapter 32
Le Métro

Taking the Métro in Paris with these morons was a lesson in the comic absurd. The whole monstrous group of unshaven, sullen Albertan cowboys looked like convicts sitting amongst clusters of nattily dressed chain-smoking Parisians, who cast us disdainful glances up from books and parcels I imagined were bought in boutiques along the Champs Elysées. Although they were magisterial rock stars in the States and Canada, the ills looked like circus carnies in Paris, staring at landmarks with slack-jawed awe. And if the ills were good friends with the Hellions at the beginning of the tour, by the time we all made it to Liège, Belgium, where we played a squatters' camp up in the hills of that drab industrial city, things quickly worsened.

There were hissy fits and conniptions after the show in Liège. An argument broke out among the ills, the Hellions and a German band, Die Fausts, about who was going to have to hitchhike to the next gig in Passau, because the cooling system on the rented van had broken down and there was no room for everyone in the other van. Burnd Blochmund of Die Fausts said it couldn't possibly be them because they were the headlining act in Passau. Clark stated coolly that it couldn't be the ills because Passau was one of the few places that we had actually garnered a core audience. The Hellions said it couldn't be them because they were the best fucking rock band anyway and the guys should be the ones to hitch-hike.

When things turned cold that night and the gear was all loaded up, everybody stood outside the van in the drizzle, looking down at the grey-blue shimmering city. I fingered the wad of German marks in my pocket and felt like absconding right then with all our money and buying a plane ticket. I wanted to curl up in a cheap hotel and fantasize about apple orchards and farmers wearing John Deere caps and acres and acres of dark green cow corn. I wanted to think about lazy hellos, red soil and tides washing in and out, sluicing up and over the salt marshes in that perfect whitewashed university town that was my home.

Chapter 33
The Diary

When we reached Amsterdam I started to write the whole sad episode down. I was no longer able to get the release I needed through venting myself in words or screaming like a rabbit at shows. I was starting to feel lonely in the company of these determined people, even if we were all similarly disenfranchised. It felt like the most natural thing to write it all down, and so I did, on scraps of paper and table place-mats and anything that I could find. I found a comfort in words, in the listing of events, and I became a hopeless addict. It was only by sitting there and scratching away that I could exorcise all those field battles and biplanes that went whizzing and buzzing like wartime sirens through my head.

> *Pigalle, Paris, November 26*
> Last night Clark and I sat in the pouring rain and talked about pulling off the perfect victimless crime, never having to work in our lives ever again. Back at the apartment the boys watch *Midnight Cowboy* and no one says anything other than Ratso is a loser and that losers attract losing and losing has an addictive beauty. Right now I've got a terrible cold and am sniffling endlessly. Ratso dies at the end of *Midnight Cowboy*. But he does eventually change his underwear.

> *Le Fiacre, Paris, November 30*
> This morning we drove to Bordeaux and I am banging my head against the dash whispering: breakdowns, breakdowns. But Clark wants no part of that. He is ignoring me, giddy, hungover, sprawled in the back seat listening to the story of Jerry waking up one morning and having a concoction of sour chocolate milk and cigarette butts poured into his eye sockets and having his body

beaten with hockey sticks. A reference to "shit tub," or shower=bidet, which means that there was never any toilet paper in the house so the occupants bent over the shower knob instead. Soon Jerry and Clark get into a punching fit on the pavement at the petrol station, the French gendarmerie bristling when Jerry says Gen-dam-er-ee in a loud voice at the cash counter. Now we're in Bordeaux in a clean tiny cellar, with the raucous French crowd up above yelling and cat-calling, and everybody is excited for the upcoming show, anticipating a responsive crowd after the apathy and ill-humour that greeted our dismal performance last night.

Club Auto Rock, Paris, Dec 7

There is a dog sleeping on my jacket at present and I am stricken with the absurd fear that if I do something wrong the man who owns it will come after me with a knife. I am also concerned that it may pee all over my coat and perhaps my leg. It's fascinated by the food that I have stored in my bag, the cheese and the sausage. It's driven by a carnal lust for food. I do wonder if my future lies in the gutter somewhere, with clever things coming out of my mouth at odd intervals mixed with sleaze and confused rambling, a release of toxins stored up over time.

Les Bleu Heures, Paris, Dec 9

It seems like Karol that bastard promoter is confused about how to do things as the rest of the band. No arrangements have been made about where to stay after the Paris show since Burnd's place is now out of the question, because Burnd's stepfather hates us. We drive for several hours all through suburban Paris while Mr. Sunglasses talks of Sally—back home in Edmonton—hassling him to buy her a Christmas present and him telling her he can't cut into his drinking money. The blur of neon seen through the window, the signs for cheap hotels, light up on the roofs of buildings. We head down Boul. Montparnasse, explaining to Karol that Clark would be happy sleeping in the van, and Burnd just turns, insulted. Burnd says he'd rather we stayed with his father than sleep in the van, and Clark spends the evening telling him that his home is a van and that he wants to sleep in the van. Eventually a compromise is reached and Jerry goes to Burnd's, Clark takes the van and I sleep on the floor at this French fuck Gwarr's place with Mr. Sunglasses stepping over me reading *Leaving Las Vegas* and playing Patsy Cline, singing "Crazy" over and over on the stereo.

Chapter 34
Uncomfortable Male Love

I knew that I loved Clark almost as much as I had loved Charlene. Not in the physical sense, though I loved his physicality. It was more that I loved his calmness and the way that he sat in the back of the van, pulled off his shirt, grinned like a shit-eater and looked like a man who appealed to women. Never in my time of loud proud talk about who may have been the better man, never in the quiet times that Clark tuned his guitar and played softly in the back did it ever occur to me that we would ever be less than friends. I admired the silly bastard for keeping his mouth shut when there was a pile of shit being talked in the van. I admired him for sitting and beating on his guitar and showing me new licks and riffs when times were getting grim. I admired him for sitting in the side seat of the van doing crossword puzzles faster and better than anyone else. And I admired him for lying in his bunk, reading and studying books like *History of War in the Balkans* and *Dark Secrets of the South Mountain* and then sitting on the edge of his bunk, yelping like a dog and quoting all the harsh parts from memory.

There was something so beautiful and good and smart and decent in the boy. I knew that I was a hopeless and immature curmudgeon with awful habits, but Clark didn't seem to mind what other people found so intolerable. So when the two of us were alone in Europe I was surprised to find that there was a vulnerability in Clark. It occurred to me that the reason we got on so well, why I had been like a moth to his flame, was because like me, Clark had no real home.

"That's the thing, eh," Clark said, drawing in the dust with a stick. "Sounds cool when yer eighteen. You get into it and it's all a cool vibe. Gettin' paid. Touring the country. Screwing hot chicks. But after a while it's the same thing. Dealing with some drunk promoter who's trying to constantly undermine you. Playing some sheet set and there's some harsh girl in the van and some sheet guy from your hometown who wants to sleep with her. And you don't know how long he's been there. But he's going, 'Cool man, you guys are the coolest' and he's drinking your beer and offering you some. Even though he's an old work friend from the cannery er whatever you have to start bad-vibing him away. It's just the sheets, generally."

Clark gripped the buckle at his waist. "This is the real ticket."

I smoothed the buckle with my fingers, traced the outlines and read the inscription:

1967
Pincher Creek Rodeo
Boys Steer Wrestling Champ

"Impressive," I said.

"Nothin' but good times on the rodeo circuit, Selwyn. I used to compete all around Pincher Creek, Taber, Lethbridge, Cardston, Raymond, Coultts. This whole rock thing's bound to die sometime. And when it does I'll just go back to the farm. I got a few acres of hills off a coulie near Coultts where I can build a house, be a recluse, play music and tend to the stock. Get back to nature...er whatever." He looked at me with his greeny eyes. Yelped.

"Howbout you cockbite?" he said.

Clark seemed so gullible. I wanted to tell him how naive and idealistic he was to think he could build a house, tend livestock and behave like some recluse when his whole life was built around people worshipping and revering him. At that moment Clark seemed the opposite of everything I had imagined him to be when we first met, the confident, true-grit caretaker of a successful rock band. In Europe he seemed uncertain, slightly empty, a pawn in the whole narcissistic rock game, fumbling for affirmation in the wake of the band's bygone success. But I didn't want to say this to him. This was something that he would never say to me. He was highly skilled at keeping his mouth shut when he knew talking was going to get him nowhere. I respected and loved that more than anything.

"I have a child," I said finally. I didn't say it for shock, I didn't say it because I was trying to impress him. I said it because everything seemed a damned fraud and I, in my self-righteousness and condescension towards him was a purveyor of that fraud. "I have a kid, I had a girlfriend and I report to an adopted mother who's going senile on me."

"You mean Bee?"

"You know of Bee?"

"You talk about her all the time, Selwyn."

"When?"

"Non-stop when drunk," Clark gulped. Got up out of his bunk.

"She sounds like a real character. Like someone you'd want to sit with for an afternoon and talk to a bit. It's no biggie, Selwyn. We all got the big load to carry around."

He looked at me. I frowned.

"Okay Clark. What do you carry around?"

Clark shrugged. "The neverending focus. The lifelong obsession and fear of bein' a thirty-five-year-old bald fat guitar player with an extreme need to be in a band. Anyone's band. Harsh." Clark shivered.

This was getting me down. "Clark we hardly laugh, anymore. All I do is moan and bitch."

"Yah but you're funny when you complain. Funny to me, anyways." Clark started tooling with his belt.

"I have to get out of this Clark. It's just not me."

Clark had that faraway, bored look again.

"What else you gonna do? Go back to the land of rocks and rain?"

"Yes."

"And do what?"

"Make amends, Clark."

"Make amends for what?"

"I've been an ass to the old dear. I'm attached to her still. I've also lied about something very bad."

"No one's perfect, Selwyn."

"Not everyone is an arsonist, Clark."

"Hah," he laughed at me, "you're pipin' 'er. You haven't got it in you to do that. Anyway, if you did, whoever you burned probably deserved it."

Clark went silent again. Moped.

"You'd be lonely as hell down there, Selwyn."

"I'm lonely here."

"Yah maybe eh." His head sank a little.

I was going crazy in the head. I needed an out. Saw it. "Why don't you sing in the band?"

"Don't have the rock voice." Clark was glum.

"I don't have the rock voice."

Clark looked at me. "You got the screech. Most guys would kill for that and you're bein' a faggot bitch about it."

"Clark..." I was stuck. "I feel lonely. I feel miserable, tired and grim."

"Just a bad day is all."

"Clark. I was raised in a house where the loudest thing was the tea kettle. I am not meant for this life. I am meant for loitering about a house in a waistcoat."

"Non digs." Clark grumbled.

"What?"

"Don't dig poor rationalizing guy." He climbed into the van and pulled a t-shirt up and over his head. "Don't dig the poor tour. Don't dig lotsa shit."

"I didn't say I would leave the tour before it was done, Clark."

Clark shuffled in his seat, didn't respond.

"I didn't say I'd leave in the middle of the tour..." I looked at Clark. Shirt over his head, nose pointing through. As much as I loved him I knew then that he wouldn't listen to me and that I had to get away from this madness that was simply not me.

Mr. Sunglasses cemented this decision for me that evening when he slunk through the room and sat on the edge of the bed trying to wake the whole crowd of us up. Then he said, "C'mon in, Tee Rez," and a woman came in, a woman with dark wavy hair and a hat that she held in her hand. She put the hat up to her mouth and stood there looking guilty, her shirt slightly open at the neck. Mr. Sunglasses took the hat from her and said, "Do you have some treats fer me Tee Rez?"

She laughed nervously and shyly. He threw the plastic and glue he was holding onto the bed. Both of them got into the bed beside me. "See that there, Tee Rez?" Mr. Sunglasses was pointing to me. "That there's the impostor."

Chapter 35

So on to Prague, knowing Clark was a fool to think I was going to tolerate even one more week of this damned European tour. On our way through the dreary coal-fire Czech countryside we rested in Pilzen, famed for its Pilsner, which was advertised on mouldy billboards on the sides of farmhouses and old steel factories.

It was I who insisted that Clark stop the van when the border guard, a thin blond man with a scar under his eye, demanded bribe money to let our convoy of vans through more quickly. Jesse grabbed the guard by the lapels of his dull green jacket and kissed him hard on his thin lips. If the other border guards had not laughed and mocked the young fool in their harsh *brezny brezny brezny* laughter, and had not been fascinated by the convoy of hostile women packed into the van behind ours, we would have all been confined to a dingy holding cell because Mr. Sunglasses had forgotten to stash his "boos" and hash back in Passau.

I tramped into a grubby beer hall and downed a cheap plate of sour goulash. I was not surprised, looking through the cracked window, to see the whole dour lot of the ills shuffle across the parking lot and into the familiar turf of the nearest petrol station, across the street. I glared at the waitress, an abrupt girl with dark-brown hair who glanced up now and then from the sink where she was washing dishes. She pointed with dripping hands towards empty but dirty tables in the back. *Prosim, Prosim, Prosim,* she barked to the groups of old men who filed in in bunches and huddled by the door.

Later the boys straggled in with handfuls of half-eaten chicken burgers and a paper bag full of Cokes for Mr. Sunglasses to mix with his vodka, which he had with him under his coat. They sat at the bar in the smoke and gloom and watched me while I soaked the last crust of bread in my food. Jesse glowered and then started scratching his fork on the table, whining about how much the place fucken' stunk.

Farther along, Mr. Sunglasses made us stop twice on the

roadside, where he staggered between great tractor trucks hauling Audis and Staedler pens and flagged down plump young Czech prostitutes, coming back to the car each time and yelling at us to drive more slowly so that he could sober up because he was too drunk to fuck. After a while he passed out and then started singing in a whispery voice while he sipped from his bottle of vodka. "Lookin' to do me a little hoorin', lookin' to do me a little hoorin'." Then he started in on me, as I huddled under a blanket staring grimly out the window in the back seat.

"Ol' whiskey tooth wants to get in on some hoorin'. C'man Selwyn when we gonna get in on some hoorin?"

When we finally arrived in Prague I collapsed onto the cobble-stoned square and waited for Karol, the promoter, who arrived late in a rusted-out orange Skoda jammed with a fat dark-haired woman and a pack of hostile kids aged three, five, six and seven. Somehow we all piled into that rusting car. Squashed in the front seat with my head pinned against my knee, I played "snap" with the youngest of Karol's kids, Magda, who passed cards through the knees of Jesse, who was sitting on my lap. The little girl put me in a good mood, there was something enchanting about her. One of her teeth was missing and she fumbled with her lip and then pointed towards my mouth. She yelled at Karol, who grunted towards his fat wife; she clapped her hands together. "My little babushka says you should brush your teeth."

Just then Mr. Sunglasses awoke, his lips against the window screen. Dirty dirty dirty dirty, he said, and the little girl took one look at him and then cradled his chin in her hand. Then she plugged his nose and mouth with her hands.

Chapter 36

The first night we played in a crummy little Irish pub run by a Canadian expatriate named Brian. When the Hellions straggled in after us, grumbling and complaining, things just got worse. The girls, their hair in dreads and tattoos down their bone-thin limbs, collapsed in a heap at the foot of the stage and smoked cigarettes and spoke in dull conspiratorial tones. Brian finally got the hint that they had a clause in their contract that said they weren't gonna be loading in any of their gear. By that point I ached in my joints, in my eyes and ears and in my back and lungs. I hovered near the back, but then little Magda came over to me and stretched her hands out in front of her. She counted as she smiled, pressing down on her fingers, "Jeden, dva, tri..." Then she stopped and thought for a moment and put her hand on my knee.

I was miserable as I looked at the little fingers, the pink dimples and the bluey plastic ring that she wore on her pointing finger. I imagined the ring as little blue booties tied tight to the feet of an infant boy in the back seat of a moving car. Magda's voice became Charlene's and I was suddenly there that night. That night in Nova Scotia when the lot of them had packed into the car and deserted me. I took Magda's little hand and held it.

"Listen to me you little monkey. Don't you ever think that your daddy doesn't love you," I said. And she looked at me.

I felt an awkwardness in my face. When I looked in the mirror, I was embarrassed to see the twisted wreck of a smile. The little girl followed me around most of the night. I finally had to pick her up and carry her back to her fat mother, who was talking with Karol and planning, amidst three other children and a group of friends, the next four days of the tour. Later I passed out on the kitchen floor at Karol's place with Magda rocking backwards and forwards on a chrome chair, watching me. With the grey sky silhouetting her curly black hair and crouched posture, she cast animal shapes across the wall as she peered at me between the gaps of her fingers.

CHAPTER 37

We arrived at Karoly Rulska in a convoy that included the rusted-out Skoda, an aging black Mercedes, the band vans and an old Austin-Healy that was driven by an old man who wore grey-goggled glasses and drank cough syrup while he drove and sang. Magda's father Karol kept announcing that the old man was Agro, the people's poet of Prague, and we could hear him in the car beside us, singing as he drove and yelling out poems written on torn-up paper. When we finally stopped, Agro stripped and ran naked through our convoy and then down another row of cars. He tore a sheet off a clothesline and waved it behind him like a sail. Using petrol siphoned from the Skoda, we saturated cabbages in a field at the side of the road and set them ablaze where they lay.

At first, the girls refused to participate because they just wanted to smoke pot by themselves. They began to warm to the idea of making a night of it all when Agro started to paint little blue flowers and birds on his shoulders and little designs on the cheeks and forearms of Nisha, who was the lead singer and ringleader of the Hellions. Then Nisha scooped a chillum into one of the charred cabbages and wrote across Agro's ass: THE STAR IS ME.

Everybody got more and more stoned as the stars beamed in the heavens but I knew that something felt wrong in me, that something felt clouded and melancholy and terrible. The Hellions began to play, slim as they were and hateful, picking at their strings, bent knees, legs on amps, rocking, in their skin tight black leotards and striped pullovers, kicking at a panting dog that roamed across the stage, spinning and grinning madly till we got right up there and hit the stage at Karoly Ruska. I took a Pilzen and sprayed it across the open mouths of the audience and then turned towards Clark, who was just standing there like a dopey scarecrow, strangely gaunt and watching it all. Then we started to play, and people held back for a while, smoky embers in the distance like fireflies, heads down, dancing in quiet appreciation till they were pushed forwards, slamming into one another. Someone began chucking food—mustard, sauerkraut, onions, rotten cabbage—into the middle of the tarpaulin. At the end it was as I knew it would be. We never finished the set. Everybody was on the tarpaulin worming and writhing till all was one shivering groaning mass expanding and imploding like a heartbeat: *ka-bump ka-bump ka-bump.* At this pathetic sight I threw the microphone down in disgust. As the band straggled away through the trees, laughing at first and then solemn, I remained for a second all alone, standing like a damned fool child with my hands up to my face, wanting to scream at them to stop. But nothing would come out of my mouth. No whimper, nothing. In that futile, miserable instant, the rabbit had finally deserted me.

I wandered behind Clark down through the trees, past Jesse, who was sitting with his elbows on his knees, mist rising from his dewy burns, past him into a clearing where I sat down on a rock, broken bottles and tin cans all around. It was there that I saw Magda leaning backwards in the moonlight, lifting her tiny little dress up over her head and then back down again, her voice high-pitched and questioning. I watched her lift her dress up then pull it down, teasing the little frills of lace and curling them as she played all alone. And then I saw Mr. Sunglasses sitting in the front seat of one of those dead Russian cars, drinking with his elbow on its rusted door. He was telling Magda to come to him and she came forwards. Then I saw Agro standing there in the darkness rubbing his stomach and blinking. I saw him stare at Magda and Mr. Sunglasses.

Mr. Sunglasses said, "Hey Selwyn. What're you doin' down here? That little girl she's a beauty, eh Selwyn, a real heartbreaker she's gonna be?"

I looked at Magda, poor little cherub, one finger in her mouth, watching everything. She was naked except for her socks and Mr. Sunglasses was drunk and smiling and miserable. Then I saw Agro, his face illuminated by the moonlight, hold a field stone high up above Mr. Sunglasses' head. Agro became white in the face. He brought the stone down over

Carl's head and then he started after me, still holding the stone in his hand. I hopped over shrubs, ducked under tree limbs and chased through the clearing and past Clark, who was lying on his back near the tarpaulin, staring at the shining sky above. I wanted to tell him that I was certain I had just witnessed a murder, but he just looked at me and smiled his dopey smile and I knew once and for all that I had no choice but to get gone.

CHAPTER 38

All I know is that right after that I was running. Everything seemed justified to me in an instant and then everything seemed pure madness again. I knew that if I ran away I would be blamed for the violence, but I could not stop myself. I panicked. I ran through the cobble-stoned streets and out into the countryside and through the lush fields and onto dirt roads, stumbling blind and burdened by what I had seen. I remember shivering in the back of a potato truck, I remember freezing on the side of an autobahn, rubbing my knees and chewing on bits of greasy sausage and rank cheese. I remember sitting frozen stiff with dirty clothes and bleeding knees in a bright and metallic airport corridor amongst a bustling crowd of backpackers, moribund Saudi sheiks and their baleful wives, and a team of fat German men.

I sat on a bench and counted my money over and over in that airport, shivering as an endless list of possibilities nagged and jabbered at me. I had a passport and five thousand dollars in saved roadie pay. I checked the giant black departures board that blinked and clicked above me and could see that there were five flights leaving Frankfurt over the course of that night. I sucked on my lip. Beat at it hopelessly. None to Canada. Not one. None to the U.S., even. New York. Boston. Nothing. But I couldn't go home. To what? Straggle up the coast. Not like this. As a coward. A defeated idiot held down with straps and hooks and a bedpan in a room in the old rectory. Dr. Günter and all those childhood shrinks and burly town clowns and Mounties and the whole village volunteer fire department hovering over me. Charlene there too. Still winsome and lovely as the day I had last seen her. I could see the faces. The looks of fear and disillusionment. Look at him. The sad sad state of him. My darling Selwyn. How are you. Stoop. Hair all down like a wave. Kiss Kiss Kiss. Wipe Wipe. Tears. I could imagine Charlene getting into bed with me when all the grown-ups had left. Pressing her breasts into me like she used to. The way I used to pinch her nipples so that they nearly bruised and the way she leaned into my ear and kissed me.

Silly girl. That silly girl I loved more than I had ever loved anything. Still I kept on sitting there in that airport, tears in my eyes, thinking of that girl. No. No. No. Soon it would be alright. I was unhappy in that band. I had to get away. Moscow. Leningrad. I huffed a bit, adjusted myself. These names sounded good. But what sorts of people? Large matronly women with oxen and woollen socks and ploughs carving slices of thick damp mud along the Volga. Teams of horrid children from little huts on plots of land running like the clappers after the fearful wretch from Canada. No. No. No. No more menacing children. I couldn't hack it. I didn't like the look of the gruff pilots I'd seen drinking in the airport lounge or the look of the shoddy AeroFlot planes that I'd seen rusting on the tarmac. Russian tanks and vodka. Solemn serious music. No. No. No. I wasn't going to be the lone Canadian that crashed into the sea with a bunch of boozy cheering Soviet soldiers in that plane.

Riyadh? Sand and callous camels. The thought of my head being lopped off and passed around like a soccer ball by children on their way to school. No. No. No. No. Defending myself in a small Arabian airport with guns pointed at me, explaining in a tense and submissive tone that I had not maimed or killed anyone and that it had been the horror of the act that had frightened me and that yes I was a coward for running but I had darling Bee in Nova Scotia who would vouch for me. God I was a nit, a silly tit of a man fidgeting and thinking out loud while I went down that list of destinations on the departures board, each one representing an immediate and frenzied escape from the panic and fear and shock that were alive and burning within me once again.

Australia? But no. It was not Australia...it was Algeria? What luck. Christ. I'd be DOA. Burned on the spot, a gaunt charred stick in a field, shrill voice still protesting everything and everyone. Afghanistan? Mules and pushcarts, AK-47s and me buried under a cloud of sand. Poor pale man with a chest like a starling, suffocating while goats and sheep bit at my clothing. Hell? Did hell have an airport runway? Might as well just skip the ballast and silliness and suck hard on the exhaust pipe of the inevitable. Hell. Hello?? What's this... Pale face, kind eyes, rosebud mouth, kimono and clogs, smiling winsome face of...

Chapter 39
Tokyo

Still Tokyo came at me like a blinding red sun over a bloated stinking sea. There I was, stalking through Ikebukuro Station, past capsule hotels and drink dispensers that dropped cold coffee in tin cans and Sapporo beer cans, into the neon flash. Starving, I bit into onigiri and sat on a street corner with a bowl of cheap noodles and poured warm tap water into the mix, stirring it with my finger. I walked through magazine shops and marveled at manga magazines, teeny-porn *Beppin* magazines, down alleyways with an ambient purple glow and into ramen shops. Waxy food was displayed in stinking stall windows, idiotic, electronic little-girl voice greetings in doorways. Irashemase. I-ra-she-ma-se. I-ra-she-ma-se.

I hesitated in the doorway of a little food shop, looking at the little stained curtain, tatami mats, pillows, salarimen, silky purple kimonos wrapped round knock-kneed women. The man at the bar, his face middle-aged, humourless, made up of lines and black spurts of hair, laughed at me while he ordered me up a round of yakitori and sake and Kirin and sake and Kirin and sake till I couldn't walk. My face was on the counter, spilling the contents of everything that I had had inside of me for the past few days, Czech potatoes and legumes, German sandwiches, ramen, noodles like guts running out of me over the counter. Still the same. I-ra-she-ma-se. I-ra-she-ma-se. The voice of a little girl, the high-pitched voice of a little girl. I closed my eyes, thinking that the voice was the voice of Magda and it was a voice I could not escape.

Chapter 40

I awoke in a kitchen, greasy walls and low gas fires and steam spritzed against the windows above me. My mouth was dry and there was a bucket beside me and a man slumped in a chair was sitting, hands on his knees, watching me. There was also a small boy of about ten or twelve curled on a cot sleeping with his face turned towards the wall. The man, I soon realized, was the barman who had served me pitcher after pitcher of beer earlier. He was wearing sandals and a sarong, leafing through a dirty magazine on the floor. He was rubbing his knuckles and staring at me with a sore look in his eyes.

An alarm clock went off. BAMP. BAMP. BAMP. The boy hit the alarm and toppled off the cot, holding his pyjamas at his waist. The father groaned something to him that came from deep in his chest and rumbled up his throat and out. The boy stepped backwards, bowed, a blend of reverence and resentfulness.

"My father he like. Suki des," said the boy.

I dabbed at my mouth with my shirt. It was wet and sore. "You understand English?"

"Engrish?" A laugh, a shy smile, an answer, a finger held inches from a thumb. "Hai so des nai. Scoshi, scoshi."

"Speak fucking English, then."

"Speak frucking Engrish. Hah."

The man groaned again and his tone seemed neither instructional nor pleased. I watched him glowering at his son. I feared the worst. "What's wrong, have you kept me here because I didn't pay for the damned beer?"

The boy surveyed me thoughtfully for some time and then turned towards his father, who had his hands folded across his chest. The father grunted and pulled a pair of baggy blue pants up over the sarong. He walked back into the bar area, through the soiled curtains and out the door into the street.

"My father says you talk too much. He doesn't like too

much talking. We say in Japan, silence is golden. But talk mouth no good. My father say uh, ano...you insultruh him. So he punched you. He like your spirit, but not your mouth, because you angry him."

"He beat me when I was drunk? God, I should have him caned."

The boy was smiling now. "Segoi," he said, "segoi. In Japan we don't have such an individual spirit. My father says he thinks you need some peace. To temple. Shinto temple. We pray and spend quiet time in Onsen, while you teach him Engrish."

"Temple?"

"My father Buddhist priest."

"The boxing Buddhist priest?"

The child watched me. "My father he want you to teach him English. In exchange he gives you holiday in tanbo. Him take care of you. You teach him about English, Western way."

"Tanbo, where's that?"

"Everywhere where there is countryside. Tanbo in Japan rice paddy. You like Japanese women?"

"Women?"

The little bastard had me. "Come," he said, pulling me along.

Chapter 41

The boy took me through a slew of bars in Rippongi, the richest and most phony part of Tokyo. I saw more sad lonely Western guys with subservient little Japanese girls on their arms than I have ever seen in war photos of Vietnam or the Second World War. There were celebrities in those bars too, tall black basketball players and svelte American actors with thin contemptuous-looking girlfriends standing beside them. Some of the homelier women drank at the counter, staring ruefully at the girls who had a lock on a famous face. Toshihiro seemed to be in awe of these men. He pointed at a blond, square-jawed boy/man sipping beer. He said the name of a famous actor, and I laughed at him. I said to Toshi, he's not *that famous person* and Toshi looked at me and grimaced in a way that I knew meant he disagreed, but was too polite to tell me that he knew I was dead wrong.

I knew then that I could have been dead wrong. It could very well have been that famous Hollywood actor. I had been away from Canada and out of contact with anyone outside the band for such a long time that I could very well now be delusional. Then, in the strangest, most imperceptible moment, the familiar bass line of "Kill The Pain" came on the speakers in the bar. There was an appreciable buzz in the air because it was the only Western song on the menu. Toshi leaned forwards and pushed towards the American movie star to ask for an autograph, which the man signed. I looked at the card he had signed and it read "Kill The Pain." I couldn't stand it anymore—that fraud singing Jeff's song, a song I had sung for far too long in Canada and all through Europe. I had to get out. OUT.

Soon we were down the street in a karaoke bar packed with whores and Taiwanese fishermen wearing dirty grey pants and soiled sweaters and American baseball caps. I sat with Toshi, his pert upturned mouth smiling in a perverted yet innocent way. In that bar I looked in the karaoke guide and found that goddamned song "Kill the Pain." Amidst the fishermen and drunken salarimen and whores with tight spandex shorts, I sang proudly in the din of red and blue flashing lights and a circling strobe, the only song I could sing:

You've got to kill the pain,
you've got to know its name
and all and all and all
that matters

Afterwards, Toshi clapped his hands together and said to everybody there, "Ano... Segoi desoka..." Then he turned to me. "Almost like the real thing, almost exactry like real thing," he said.

I tried to tell him, tried to insist that I had sung that song for five months and I had very nearly made that song my own, put my own personal stamp on it, but he just said over and over almost like real thing and laughed at me.

We were drunk again and it was early morning when we ended up in a topless bar, bottles of Jim Beam and C.C. and Stoli lined up like soldiers on the racks behind the counter. There were two Thai girls on stools on either side of me, reaching down into my pockets and grabbing me where I was alive. One whispered in my ear *my mama-san own tris prace* and the other kissed me on the neck. Then I was on the street corner looking at a taxi driver who was sitting in the front seat of his baby-blue cab wearing white gloves pulling at his fingers. He was waiting for Toshihiro, who finally came outside, holding the front drawstring of his pants like he had in the bar the night before in the company of his old man.

Chapter 42

I knew as soon as the tiny well-muscled men came in their black thick belts and wide-brimmed plastic metal caps, with their direct and solemn stares and boots clicking against the floor, that they were there for me. I had known for a while that my time was coming, as there had been a news report in one of the English newspapers shortly after I had arrived that mentioned a band incident outside Prague. I was mad with panic when I first learned of it, and I paid off a few louts to make queries for me. I quickly learned that Mr. Sunglasses had been maimed, not killed. My terrible fear that he was dead began to fade away, though I still had no proof that it had not been me who had done the maiming. My detainment in my Japanese cell lasted two years. I was not, however, maltreated by any of the other criminals with whom I was housed. Some were Taiwanese sailors and Filipino swindlers and one of them was an ugly Canuck from Saskatchewan who had made his way through Bangkok, the 7-Eleven and slut-trumpeting back alleys of Phat Pong and the wild lush countryside of northern Thailand. He talked in a slow nasal drone—slow enough to irritate but fast enough so that it was difficult to interrupt—the dead Thai coastline Koh Tao Chinese work pants and bronzed bodies and rotten coconuts and bleached crab parts and dark swirling sky with the glitz of video games and cameras flashing and dead pigs and markets of cherries and crushed frogs and tanks of fish business business business and men yelling "You get out my store."

It was around this time that I sank into a depression, a coughing, retching malaise of the soul, while the Canadian government lobbied the Japanese government to extradite me. Of course I never admitted to hitting Mr. Sunglasses, though I did confess, finally, to the interviewing officers in a mental hospital in Japan, that it had been me who had burned Charlene's house to the ground. I went through interview after interview, test after test, till eventually I had the entire detective staff in fits.

> Question: Did you intend to maim Carl Winters?
> Answer: Winters in Maine? Curling is for the Briar.
> Question: Have you ever consulted a psychiatrist?
> Answer: Have you ever consulted a podiatrist? I can smell your gamey feet from here.
> Question: Where were you on the night of May 16?
> Answer: Throwing stones at Jerry O'Reardon.
> Question: Is this Jerry O'Reardon part of the ills?
> Answer: Jerry O'Reardon wishes ill on all of mankind.

It went like that for several months. I grew despondent and thin. Then, one day, one of the arresting officers came to my room. He had in his hand a postcard that had a picture of the ills on it. On it was written:

> Japs,
>
> Listen here you Japs it wasn't that whiner Selwyn what did this to me, but a stone fell out the sky. Best part about this hospital, Selwyn, is when I see a nurse leaning over me more times than not she's twins.
>
> Singed, larC

"There," I pointed at the note, "vindication. Carl is alive and this note proves that it wasn't me."

More sharp inhaling from the hospital staff, hunched dark heads shaking and scratching in the pad. "Suut. Suut. Ano. Muscoshi. Wakaranai."

The interpreter came forth from the huddle. "This is fan mail?"

"No Jesus," I said, standing up out of bed, "this is a letter from Carl. He's saying it wasn't me that maimed him. Don't you understand?"

"Ah. Wakarimashta." The interpreter looked enthused and went back to the fold. More of this "Suut. Suut." Head shaking. Sharp inhaling. "Ano Wakaranai." The interpreter came back, looking grim.

"But investigating officer say weapon field stone, not tree stone. This man very damage man."

"Look," I gripped the edge of the bed. "I want out. O-U-T." I stood up. And then the men came at me, thumbed my forearm and jabbed a needle in my vein.

Chapter 43

Eventually it was decided that I was mentally unfit to stand trial. I was released into the care of Toshihiro's father, the Buddhist priest who had contacts with the Japanese underground, the Yakuza. The agreement was that I would continue to tutor the old man in English, which I was pleased to do as I assumed that it meant that I would remain alive for some time. I had no idea what else the Buddhist priest had in store for me. I was suspicious of everyone who was around me. I felt powerless. To keep me company, a Canadian filmmaker stayed with us for several months while he conducted interviews and gave his documentary—originally a music tribute to the ills traveling through Europe—an entirely new Japanese/Yakuza focus. I remember little about that time other than how the documentary filmmaker became fascinated by the underworld figures that the Shinto priest was connected to—mainly thugs and housewives and young boys who beat each other silly from time to time.

Eventually the whole pack of us traveled south. It was decided that I should convalesce and keep teaching the Buddhist priest English; the filmmaker could finish compiling footage for his documentary. I was especially pleased because I had a friend in the filmmaker. We talked at great length about the absurdity of my confinement and about his own children, of whom he spoke fondly. He was especially fascinated to learn of the origins of the rabbit shriek, as his own kids were having some trouble at school. As I talked to him I started to realize that my own situation as a child, apart from the fact that I had been abandoned in an apple orchard, had not been entirely unique. The filmmaker's kids had invented an entire language of dissent based on the frogs and tadpoles that they found in a neighbourhood pond. The filmmaker stayed another four months and when he returned to Toronto he maintained a correspondence with the rector's wife. He tried his best to clear my name with my old friend the cowboy, who wrote me but one postcard, postmarked Edmonton.

Selwyn,
Carl don't talk much sense these days. But he sure makes a hell of a roadie.
CLARK

Chapter 44

I stayed in Makabe, our village in southern Japan, for ten years and married a Japanese girl. I learned to speak Japanese fluently and to enjoy sakura, the spring cherry blossoms, the armoured kendo contests and fugi nagashi, the brightly painted fish streamers that hung from poles outside the villagers' homes. I learned to enjoy the sounds of the evening, shimmering crickets and croaking amphibians in the luxuriant summer tanbo and the white swans which swam in manicured gardens. I learned that I had a patience for these people, that I could lose myself in this culture because everyone was polite and distant and knew when to leave me alone. And though I became known as gaikokogin, or an acceptable foreigner, and became a fixture in the rural parts of Okayama, I knew my place in this adopted soil, for I would always be an outsider who shadowed their landscape.

I lived with my Japanese bride in a rural part of Makabe in a small house that I rented from the Shinto Priest. I kept a garden of cabbages and carrots and corn and on the periphery of this place I planted apple trees from seeds that I had asked the rector's wife to send to me. I then began a three-year period where, under the old Japanese man's guidance, I began to paint landscapes. Japanese cranes standing stiff in the rice fields, ornate wooden hillside temples with fluttering white prayer wheels all around, moon-faced kids in blue-and-black uniforms jumping rope in the dusty schoolyard. Mayumi, my wife, became my model, and I fell into this craft and began to marvel at just how good at it I was. I painted Mayumi in traditional colourful Japanese garb, sitting in the garden sun of the recently flooded field, her mouth full and mirthful. I painted her with men: her father, a wizened old sensei, wearing his formal Buddhist garb, and her brother, a local policeman, posing and flexing his muscles in the parking lot of the community centre.

While I called Mayumi my wife and we conducted our affairs as a married couple, I knew nothing about her for she had come to me as chattel, with the house. All I knew of this woman was what I had been told by the Buddhist priest: Mayumi had worked as a hostess in a bar, her mother was a Filipino whore who had once been his mistress, and while she was a pretty and kind girl she was also stupid and predictable like all women who traded their bodies for yen.

During the years that I painted and painted, I picked away at the mystery that was this woman with whom I shared a futon on the floor of our tatami room. Our courtship had been brief. At first we were cold with each other. She acted in a way that was consistent with the Japanese people I had met. She was forever polite, doting in a way that was both reserved and highly skilled. She served me my lunch of sour pickle and rice, green tea and sashimi. I would take the food and eat it slowly and deliberately, for it took me a great deal of time to get used to seaweed and raw fish. She would watch me from afar, then eat when I had finished, alone, in her quarters, sitting down with her chopsticks in her hand, scooping at her rice and noodles like she had ice cream and a spoon.

She never let on that she was bitter or hateful about having to serve a complete damned stranger. It wasn't long after she had been forced on me that I followed her into her tiny room, an adjunct to the main room where I slept. I knelt down beside her where she ate. She looked at me from behind her painted white face and got up and scurried towards the corner away from me. After a time of my chasing her she grew tired of this stupid game and sat there, eating and staring at me somewhat emptily. I would try to touch her face and she would politely withdraw from me. I would persist, drawn forth like a child examining a picture of a naked woman for the first time. I would try to rub my finger along her face, traces of white makeup like chalk against my finger. She would gather her little kimono up at her knees and place her hand at her head, then run outside and squat at the patio and turn her head away from me.

I would get angry and try to tell her to leave: I would yell, pointing my hand down the dirty little path with the creek running past, for her to get out. Then I would kick at something in anger and frustration and I would catch my toe and it would swell like a little blue balloon and she would laugh. Slowly we began to share a language of finger-touching and drawing, of invented nods and phrases mouthed as we knelt on the tatami mat. As this coy vocabulary of glances and postures improved and our confidence with each other grew, I gained my first inkling of the Japanese tongue, a child's Japanese, spoken in a simplistic giddy game that children use when playing with each other.

She would tease me, announce with her hand over her mouth when she had finished eating a fat Japanese peach: "Dekita, Dekita!!! I'm finished, I'm finished." I would behave very solemnly and seriously. "Wakatta! Wakatta! I understand I understand." We began to share secrets with one another, dark secrets that marked our pasts. We laughed and giggled beneath the covers as she grabbed me and I slipped inside her, speaking Japanese and English and little soft lies and whispers. I tucked her hair behind her ears, kissed her lips and then she rose on me like a Japanese cowgirl, red booties and all.

I fell in love with Mayumi because I was a child with her. I was allowed to be innocent and naive and stupid and there was no charade of trying to be clever or coy or diffident or insensitive or any of that damned withdrawn nonsense. We were like two children learning our smells, our likes, our hates and our fears. It was as if we were hoisted aloft in a balloon, sipping green tea and staring down at a jammed landscape of flashing lights and dark skies and cars on highways like blood swimming through arteries. There were stadiums with crowds of fifty thousand holding banners and noisemakers, cheering on the Yomiuri Giants vs. the Seibu Lions. The whole world became like a dream: washed-up American ballplayers strutting around the field beside Fujitsu Motor Company signboards. Mayumi and I drowsy, like we were opiated and just floating there looking down at everyone.

Of course, it didn't last. After a few years had passed, I began to realize that this utter floating and loss of self were a kind of sloth and madness. Elements of my cautious, defensive, paranoid self came back in ways that hurt Mayumi. I made her cry and question me and retreat to her room alone. I would escape on my push bike through the farmers' fields, through the tanbo and to the Shinto temple, where I would sit on the banks of the property blowing on a piece of grass between my thumbs. I sank into a period of reflection and regularly cancelled my English lessons, and very soon my despondency and inactivity caused the Buddhist priest to summon me again, this time for counselling.

For two or three weeks I instructed Mayumi not to answer the phone when it rang. I spent a great deal of time away from the house but it was no good. I was scared of the Buddhist Priest/Yakuza because he had constructed a whole idyllic life for me, and I had fallen into it so easily. I knew he was the master of me and that I was powerless and hopeless and that he could just as easily take my comfort away as grant it. Then, late one Friday afternoon, a delinquent lad of eighteen or nineteen arrived at my house in a modest white Toyota Crown. He wore Wayfarers and opened the car door, revealing silky purple track pants and a dyed red stripe in his hair.

"Remember me?" he said. "My name Toshihiro."

Chapter 45

The room to which I was summoned was a café, where I saw middle-aged bluntish men smoking King cigarettes and sipping from tins of Suntory chilled coffee, at plastic tables with block prints of dragons and birds and streamers and warriors on the walls signed with Kangi characters like flits of paint. I was surprised to see on one carefully lit wall, some of my own paintings of Mayumi, her painted Kabuki mask, her early-morning rituals of combing her hair in our bedroom and dusting the patio outside with her whisk broom. Another of Mayumi making a small fire on the hillside, playing with a small kitten peering from out of an abandoned tire. Another painting depicted a family of ducks feeding on the weeds that grew between the supple rice stalks. Farther along, my paintings looked crude and preposterous next to the florid strokes of the Buddhist priest's collection of stolen masterpieces by Monet, Matisse, Cézanne, which were grouped in bright bunches of three and four. Farther down on the velvet-draped walls, near tables lit with small blue and red candles, hung moody Renaissance paintings by Flemish Masters. Bowls of ripe fruit with moths fluttering overhead, yellowing pears and dead pheasants and glasses of burgundy wine, little worms and insects hidden in the glare of the finish, all of it stolen from galleries, private collections, basements, museums.

When the Buddhist priest had watched me for some time as I stared at this remarkable assemblage of art, he summoned me to sit with him at his table, where he was flanked by three young men. One of them was Toshihiro, a red stripe in his hair, smiling broadly yet still deferring towards me as was the custom.

"Gaikokogin," said the Buddhist priest, "my aides tell me," and with this the two young lieutenants on either side of the Yakuza man swelled with pride and conviction, "that you are unhappy here and have not just run away from a group of friends but also from your own true family."

"I don't have any damned family," I protested. But it was then I saw his eyes widen. The furrows deepen.

"Dame des. Dame des. Bakayaru."

The Buddhist priest drummed his fists on the table and for the first time I could see the blue tattoo on his chest rise up his neck. He barked at his interpreter, a short wiry man who had large spectacles and cleared his throat nervously. The man came forwards and took me by the arm.

"Gaikokogin," began the interpreter, "in the five years that the master has known you he has welcomed you and given you a life in Japan that any citizen would wish for. You live with a beautiful wife, you have a generous country house, you can live and work freely and you have a benefactor who will buy your art and keep you in good stead."

"And I am thankful for that," I said.

More barking and drumming on the table from the priest/Yakuzaman.

"Dame des." The interpreter paused. He watched the exchange between myself and the Shinto priest and removed a picture from a cookie tin. A cookie tin?? I looked at the picture.

"Trisplace."

It was a photograph of a great clay nose jutting into the sea. Orchards. Apple blossoms in the foreground. Dark red barns. Cape Blomidon?

"No," I said, "I want nothing to do with that place. There is nothing there but sermons. And the parish newsletter that needs to be distributed every week. And fire departments. And old men in white gowns with pencils. And religion."

The old Yakuza man blinked his eyes as the interpreter muttered and grunted towards him. This time the priest came forwards and spoke. I noted with a certain amount of amazement that his pronunciation was slow, but very clear and exact for a man who had begun learning English at sixty. "This religion," he clasped his hands together, "this is what ails you?"

I was defensive now. The paranoia welled. I stood up on the chair, pointed at him.

"Don't talk to me of religion. You are a known gangster who recruits children into your miserable fold and cuts off fingers and kills people during the day while bowing down to a peaceful Buddha at night."

The interpreter came forwards again. He relieved me from the chair. We all went walkies. As a grumbling collective.

"Let's talk of this religion and the uncertainty that you emit in your own personality and work," said the interpreter, as some of the older men, and hangers-on, circled round. "Your art, for example. It worships the landscape—pictures of trees and animals and people. Everything that you do is rooted in the countryside. Your religion and the love that you feel is rooted in your art, in your expression of the human. Our Zen religion understands this..."

I tried to pull away from the persistent assistant.

"But you" I said, "the practitioner of Zen and enlightenment, are a murderer. You talk about inner peace, Wabi and Sabi, but you still don the sacramental garb of a highly respected Zen master and recruit young delinquents to break bones and whore with the best of them."

The Zen master talked to the interpreter in a very low-toned and serious conversation. The interpreter returned. He said in his most careful and precise voice: "Morality is regulative. Art is creative. This is where you are torn. Your artistic self holds your moral upbringing in contempt. You are confined and restricted by the walls within which you must express yourself. You live in perpetual torment. Here," he grabbed me, "look at your painting..."

The painting was a crude early portrait of Mayumi, her hair whipped in an evening storm, the sky all red and blue like a bruise.

"They are dark moody portraits filled with your emotions: loss, rancour, envy, happiness, bitterness, rage."

He took me farther down past the sunny optimistic Matisses, past the Monets, to the dark Flemish Masters.

"These paintings are moral. Examine the themes of corruption and evil, the moth, hovering, about to plant her destructive eggs, the worm writhing into the shiny red core of the apple, the fly buzzing. All of the images go back to Adam and Eve. They speak of corruption, the impregnation of evil. Zen has no such restrictions or determinants. It is about the self, getting to understand the self, being as one, alone. That is why your art flourishes here. There is no one to tell you what you cannot do."

"But where is the enlightenment in one fool talking to himself?" I demanded. "The Zen master is no more intelligent than a crazy person babbling to himself on the park bench." I was becoming irritated. "One seems like a damned lonely place to be. Two seems to be more desirable. Two people, opposite halves acting as one. Like, for example, two people in love."

"You can't escape it," said the interpreter, "you speak in moral terms. You feel guilt and embarrassment for your behaviour, deride yourself for feeling guilt, for expressing how you truly feel. These are the manifestations of a rigidly governed religious culture. However, both morality and art are aspects of the healing process that you must undergo within."

The Zen master adopted the tone that he had used when he had spoken to the interpreter. The interpreter listened and returned. "The thrill of stimulus cannot sustain what it is that you need. I have tried to teach you this lesson so that you can have some peace in your heart."

Chapter 46

The old man lowered his head and the unruly teens known as Yankees and delinquents and old fat men dispersed. He handed me a cassette, somewhat tiredly. At that moment he looked nothing like a murderer to me, nor like an apostle of the great oneness, nor like a man who had any great power or particular charm. The old man's eyes were crinkled and tired and I could see on his lips and in his skin a kind of terrible blue colour like you sometimes find in frozen meat. When I pressed the cassette tape into the tape deck I listened to scratchy silence and laboured breathing. When a voice finally began to speak I recognized the tone as distinctive of the Annapolis Valley. The low self-conscious voice was countrified, like a farmer or a plummer down home:

Selwyn, you don't know me from a hole in the wall but the name's Earl Stapleton and we're a name down here in canned foods: applesauce, beets, tomatoes, peas and diced carrots. You might even recognize the name from the Co-op stores that stock our product from Digby all the way up to Glace Bay. Now what I'm about to tell you is gonna come as a hell of a shock but yer childhood sweetheart Charlene is getting married to someone you well know and old Mrs. Davis is getting moved into a nursing home. There's talk about them developing that rectory land into a subdivision and I can tell you that that ain't going over too well in these parts. Now, Selwyn, as sure as my name is Earl and as sure as my company will remain in this family for generations to come, what I'm about to tell you is that I know why it was you were left in that apple orchard near on thirty-seven years ago.

Pause.

I froze, tipped forwards. The Buddhist priest held the pause button.

I nodded towards him.

It's real complicated Selwyn like things get when they don't get spoken about. The truth of the matter is that yer true mother lives down here and has lived here since you were a small boy. Now to go into things and give you the family background that yer gonna need to understand this I'll have to start by telling you that us Stapletons doesn't come from a pile a money. We are a family of two sisters and five brothers and we're one hell of a lot of close with one another. Now Alice was the older of the two sisters and the practical and stubborn one in the family who was determined to marry rich. Well she married ol' Myron Keddy of the Keddy's Transport Company and lived up there on the North Mountain in a real nice-lookin' property overlooking Hall's Harbour. But your mother, Selwyn, was another story altogether. She was some terrible dreamer, known valley-wide for her good looks and her unstable temperament. She was easily flattered and was teased and pursued from an early age. Now the thing was, Alice and your own mother got themselves knocked up around the summer of '64. Course when the girls found out, Alice was as happy as a pea in a pod. She was married, had some financial stability, and she had a man she wasn't about to leave. But your own mother and the feller that got her pregnant, Jim Lockhart, had less than a dollar to their name at any given time. But your mother loved that damned fool, couldn't get enough of him when they was young. She'd take him down to the States every summer, where he used to holiday in Old Orchard Beach in Maine and then the both of them would winter in a cluttered house up there on the Wooval ridge. When your aunt Alice gave birth, a terrible thing happened. The boy came out blue, dwarfed and stillborn. Well yer Aunt Alice went into shock right away and told Myron right there and then to take the baby out to the kitchen and run warm water over it in the sink till he brought it back revived. Now rich uncle Myron was in a panic. His wife, who had been trying to have a baby for nearly three years, had passed out in the bed, her face white like a sheet, her bed clothes all mussed and soiled. So Myron he got on the phone and called the hospital where your mother was in labour with her twins. Now your mother, swollen and tired and scared shitless about havin' kids, was talking a mile a minute into the hospital phone. She was patting her tummy and pounding her hands on the bed by her sides. Well, Selwyn, she didn't just think she was going to have twins, she figured she was gonna have triplets and she took the phone and yelled back at yer Uncle Myron, "What do you mean the baby died? Well why don't you just have one of mine. No one will be any wiser!" And so in that frantic and awful hour when time just seems to freeze, it was decided that one of them children was going up to sister Alice, while she was comatose in her bed at home. Well Selwyn in that tiny hospital room with the clock just a-tickin' your uncle Myron promised a job to old Doctor Crause's son Eldon, who was halfway to reform school before he hit his thirteenth year. The nurse, holding a promissory note to keep her own mouth shut, was sent out on a little run to the upper part of the Varneys' orchard where, it was agreed, you would be left in a quiet spot, where the Gravenstein apples grow in rows. Well Selwyn Davis, as the nurse took you through the doors of the hospital, your mother took one last lonely look at your dear little scrunched-up face and had a change of plans and started to scream: No No No. What if that baby dies out in the cold? You can't take my little man. You can't take my little man. You can't take away my little man! But it was already too late. You were in the car with the nurse hurtling across the Cornwallis dykes screeching like a banshee for your mother's milk and zipped tight into a hockey bag in the back of the nurse's truck that belonged to her boyfriend who played Junior B hockey in Hants County. You were driven up over the bumpy, pot-holed road, pulled out of the back seat by the handles of that hockey bag and squeezed into the space between the apple barrels beneath a sky that was clear and cold as Remembrance Day. You started screaming the second you were plucked from the car, while the nurse backed out in a panic and drove out through the pear and big Gravenstein trees, spinning her tires and sending dandelions and grass and clover all across the road. Meanwhile Uncle Myron was gunning down the North Mountain in his ol' Dodge Polaris and heading out through Canning and down towards the port. It just so happened that old Mildred Varney, a light sleeper, stirred in her poster bed, reached over and switched on the bedside table light. "Did you hear a damned car run out a here?" she called to her husband, who was asleep in front of the hockey game. "Clayton," Mildred yelled to her halfwit son, who lived in the room next to theirs, "you go on git down there and see what the hell just went on." Well Selwyn I'm old now and I never married or ever had sons er nothin', but every year all of us meet down home at the cottage and talk about ol' times. Well when we all heard that Charlene was marrying finally and that old Gwendolyn was being put in a nursing home and that you was being blamed for a sin most terrible, my old heart couldn't take the silence no more and I figured I was gonna tell you what no one else down here got the guts to say and that is that you were that little boy in the orchard and that Charlene Lockhart is your sister. Selwyn, you two are twins.

Twins?

I knew the second the cassette went in that I had to get home and finally face the women who had given me up. Marlene. No way in hell was I going to let Bee die in a nursing home and let all the rectory antiques get auctioned off to worthwhile charities while I learned of some dimwit schoolteacher or travelling salesman who had moved into my childhood home and mowed down the rectory flowerbeds. No. I was going home. Home. Home. Home. Home. The words were as natural to me now as they had been alien for years before.

Suddenly I swelled with rage and resentment and a peculiar sense of pride at being briefed on the very intimate details of this place that I came from. If I was going home, though, I wasn't going home on anyone's terms but my own. I was going home with Mayumi, staying at a neutral location, a hotel or a bed and breakfast, in Halifax or someplace down the valley, and visiting them all on the day of Charlene's wedding. The fact that she was getting married was enough to floor me, but my regret was crushed by the thought of what my having been intimate with my own sister meant. It was a sadness, a regret, a void, a longing for this all to be finally resolved. But it wasn't guilt or shame. I had no idea and it had been a case of unfortunate and mistaken circumstances. But what of those who had known?? How could they have let this go on?

I was also angry that I had not had the temerity to seek out my own parents, when it was something that I had felt burdened by since I was a small child. I felt angry at Bee for not telling me that she was gravely ill and at myself for letting the years slide by and not thinking of anyone but myself. Goddamn. Goddamn. Goddman. I was swearing as I came out of that café, counting in my hands the money that I had to my name. Was it enough to get me to the dreary old Maritimes? Ku ju cen man yen, nine hundred thousand yen, ten thousand dollars. Money which, as always, meant nothing. Just figures, enough to buy plane tickets out of the Kansai airport. Shinkansen tickets. Ramen, hotels, beer.

CHAPTER 47

In the last year or so Mayumi had settled into being the Mayumi I knew she would be when the romance and the late nights and the English lessons wore off. Ten years on and she was practical now, a confident woman who told me what she wanted. She would scratch down the details of what groceries and amenities would cost in organized little kangi characters on pinky-brown writing paper, with pillowy teddy bears fronting billowy clouds and cutesy English phrases that made no sense at all:

the loving of our time is the pleasant things

calls of the wild in the children's playful sunshine

These phrases stuck out at me like cuss words in the rector's sermons. Trying to explain to Mayumi why this Japlish made no sense was futile. She knew more about English grammar, with her simple Japanese education, than I, with only an ear for words, could explain. Still, I tried to show her that English was a language that had evolved over time, and that those who spoke it learned from speaking it. That it was a bastard mutation of Latin, French, German and Dutch and that it was nearly impossible to explain why through and do and blew sounded the same, while though and slough were completely different.

Over time our lovemaking slowed, her little childlike giddy laugh disappeared, but I grew to respect her in the quiet hours that we spent in the evenings and early mornings. She told me that she loved me but that I was an outsider in her country, that I would never be forgiven for what my great-grandparents had done in Hiroshima and that, though I was Canadagin, I would never be thought of as anything but a noisy Yank. Old men would smile at me, but it was a fallacy, just the veneer of this society, for they would always whisper the same thing: "Bakayaru, bakayaru." There goes the bastard. There goes the bastard. There goes the bastard.

So I was relieved to come home. The Yakuza/Buddhist priest agreed to let me go in exchange for keeping the bulk of my paintings. Mayumi, who was in the kitchen pouring rice into the rice cooker, greeted me with a wayward, concerned glance when I arrived home. The rice spilled down over her hands and spattered across the floor. When she saw me she knew that I was peeved. She was shaking and trembling as she sat down.

"Look," I said, "I've got to get home to Canada and I'm not leaving here without you."

Mayumi started to sob I felt pangs of guilt begin to twinge.

"Going home. It doesn't mean forever." I tried to soothe her. "It's just like here anyway. Lots of fields, fruit trees, hills, the country. It's just the same, really just exactly the same as Japan."

Mayumi dropped her chin into her chest. She became silent and pouted.

"Please don't pout, Mayumi. I need you, need you in my life. I need you with me, can't you see that?" She looked at me. I wondered if she could understand everything I said.

"Wakaranai." She shook her head from side to side. Her eyes dark little twinkles.

"Canada. On-a-gi des. It's just the same really. They're very similar you know."

She patted her stomach, looked at me.

"Sick stomach Mayumi-chan?"

"Pregnant," she said, in perfectly eloquent English.

Chapter 48

Here I was all of thirty-seven with two children in the world, one on the way and one almost twenty. Was this going to be the pattern of my life, getting women pregnant but leaving shortly after because they couldn't stand me and I couldn't stand them? Was I going to be cursed with a string of unhappy children spaced twenty years apart calling me from every part of the globe, inveterate half-breeds, trying to fill some emotional gap? I could just imagine one of them now, a ghostly white, scruffy-haired, narrow-chested wastrel. Fifteen years old, tall and gangly, as unattractive as an oil-slicked bird. Dad, is that you Dad? Tell me a little about yourself, would you please? What's your emotional state generally? Is my whiny unhappy side the part that I inherited from you or is it the impatient, angry, volatile side? Oh c'mon now, Dad. Dad, you there Dad? Don't hang up on me, Dad. Dad. Dad. Dad?

And me sixty years old, sitting in my study, filled with half-read history books and biographies and literature, half-finished paintings, unframed photographs, scraps of quotes and sayings littering the floor of a house paid for by the sum left to me by the rector's wife or some anonymous patron. I would sit there, mortified at another call from another anonymous son. If not a son, then a daughter. Given my genes I was bound to spawn a tall, impossibly remote, attractive teen who spent the bulk of her time in the library, giving the boys fits and sexual conniptions because she was frigid, or hateful, or morose. A terrible cold reluctant way about her too, little disdainful shakes of the head. Just get away. Just get away. Just get away from me.

In some ways it also seemed that I had become less clever as I had gotten older, with no sense of panache or humour, no conviction to save my life. At thirty-seven I was no clever-clogs who through shrewd and clever decision-making had determined which was the surest and most invigorating life path to take. Instead, I was a wreck of a man, ravaged by the terrible knowledge that I was no better than anyone. Where I had once been a hostile and lonely child, sure that I was superior to the bulk of those who shared the world with me, I was now a weak, misguided, angry, emotional fool, a prime candidate for a life of standing naked on a cold hospital floor, waving my gown like a handkerchief. My whole life was littered with mistakes and poor decisions, venomous battles, all made in states of rash emotion. I had witnessed the maiming of a man with whom I had shared a search for meaning. I had hardly said a kind word to the old woman who had raised me. I had considered all people mean-spirited and self-serving. I had considered myself the honest one when in fact I had just plain lied. It all seemed so damned clear that I was wrong, that the my birth and my life were all wrong. My father was selfish, my mother an emotional cataclysm. There I was, sitting in someone else's house in the southwest corner of Okayama, with a dutiful wife who loved me, was pregnant by me.

It occurred to me that the Annapolis Valley, with its red clay soil and fertile valleys and ritualistic cleansing flow, was a womb. A woman's womb. A woman's womb that beckoned me.

Chapter 49

Mayumi chose to come with me. She helped me pack our things in little boxes tied with string and carefully placed pastel bow ties on the packages and painted ornate little happy faces on their sides. I did not voice the contempt I felt in handling these garish packages, for Mayumi had a deft hand at dishing out the silent treatment at her whim.

So we boxed up everything that we could and scrubbed the tiny kitchen, the hot plates, the mould from the plastic grooved tiles in the tiny bathroom. We shampooed the rug, mended the clothesline, painted the ceiling, dismantled the furniture, reapaired holes in the walls, gave away the food—ramen packages, seaweed, popcorn, cans of cola. We sold the rice cooker, the tiny ironing board, the iron and the radio, and dropped the key off with the Buddhist priest. We mailed everything at the post office down the street, everything that is but the garish little boxes that Mayumi insisted on passing to me.

"Presents for Bee," she said in a reverential tone.

"What's in them?" I asked.

"Sashimi, wasabe, soy sauce. You know, Japanese trings."

"That's very kind of you," I said abruptly, "but she's English. And she's dying. She'd probably like fruit, a tin of sweets, something like that."

Mayumi blinked at me again. Struck fear in the core of my heart.

"No show respect to mama?"

This floored me and I knew the little beauty was right. "Well whatever you give her," I corrected myself, "I'm sure she'll like."

Chapter 50

Mayumi had never travelled in an airplane before. She celebrated the morning we left with an impromptu photography session outside amongst the sparse trees, the singing frogs, the luxuriant tanbo, the flapping fish streamers. Then she went back inside and took pictures of every part of our now empty house. I posed with the Buddhist priest, Toshihiro and the clutch of bright-haired Japanese delinquents known as the Yankees. But despite the formality of the occasion and indeed the excitement, I managed to take Mayumi aside and convince her to wear a t-shirt and sweat pants instead of her best kimono for the eighteen-hour flight from Osaka to Toronto.

Going through security, she held fast to her purse, which contained a note of every size in Japanese yen. She refused to pass it to the security guard, who explained in a stern voice that he was not stealing her money, but rather protecting the security of the people on the flight. She then proceeded to giggle, laugh and blush when the security woman ran the humming metal detector around her back and down over her flat Japanese ass. When she arrived on the plane, Mayumi became very calm and observant, inspecting the seat for bread crumbs before she sat down. She listened with cocked ears to announcements from the Japanese stewards, who alternated between perfectly accented English and pleasantly cultivated Kansai dialect. She was like a little child, giddy one moment, pensive the next, unsure perhaps, slightly manic, and that mania was desirable to me—a normal place to be.

Chapter 51

I leaned past Mayumi and her tiny body curled in the seat like a cat and stared down at the landscape of Canada with feelings I could only assume were the natural skepticism and fear of a prodigal son returning home. Instead of seeming like pillows, or bedding, the clouds outside seemed watery and cold; the last place I would want to float through. The land itself, even the water just seemed cold. Tiny tiny white-capped waves rushed past under me, and the thought of me crashing in this, of the plane falling into this, seemed so unjust that I was filled with a terrible sadness. When Newfoundland appeared with its stark jutting rocks and severe landscape, I could only see the greenness. Little grassy stalks between rocks and clapboard houses, harbours and piers on the coastline, all stark whites and greys and blues.

I held Mayumi's hand, really gripped her hand, and she murmured a few times in a contented way like a little child who is safe in the arms of its parents. I didn't tell her that I had no strength left in me, that she might even come to hate this tin- bucket town more than I ever had. I didn't warn her that she might even be subjected to ridicule, to racism and the effrontery that greets those who are not from the land of Canaan. Instead I looked at her and thought of little Magda, sweet little Magda watching me and evaluating all with her shrewd little voice pitches and finger counting. Then I brought my blanket behind my head and listened to the roar of the airplane, its soporific roar, and the roar of the conversations of the people sitting in the seats behind me.

Chapter 52

The sadness soaked into me and weighed me down. I was a nervy mess wandering through the terminal in Toronto. The teeming masses of East Indians and giggling Japanese girls with braided Anne of Green Gables hair, wearing Native Canadian sweaters; fat men with sombreros and Mexican tans and Muslim women in veils and head scarves shielding naughty children from the "DO NOT ENTER" signs in the brightly lit corridors of the arrivals lounges. I just walked along, holding Mayumi's hand, thinking that I was almost home, watching everything like some invalid voyeur. What Mayumi thought of all this I could hardly know. I was too absorbed in myself and afraid of the changes that this re-entry was awakening in me. My earlier fits, the terrible tantrums and the screaming, the angst-filled outbursts, were now feeble grunts. The fits had been beaten out of me in the two years that I had spent in jail and the three years that I had spent learning to paint and I now realized that I was vulnerable in every detail. I was a middle-aged man, still thin, still faintly handsome, but the bones inside me were crumbling bones, wrapped in a youngish skin. I had bad-mouthed nearly everyone who had entered my life and had charmed, in a kind of brutal way, those same people. Yet in the long term I had nothing. My fire had died. I was rubble, the smoke and ash had settled long ago.

Chapter 53

Mayumi and I sat in the departures lounge in Terminal 3, way down at the end of an impossibly long, poorly lit corridor. We moped for a while, surrounded by families of tired-looking Maritimers and wisps of snotty-looking Torontonians making their way down east for a film shoot. Slack-eyed, bored stares, bodies half- lounging in the black vinyl rows of seating, hands scraping under seats for stuck gum, exclamations of discontent, hands over yawning faces . Fingers re-sorting wallet contents were viewed with scorn by immaculately attired men with neatly trimmed facial hair and women in black leather coats, glaring over the tops of laptop computers or looking over their leather-wrapped cellular phones. Occasionally one of the tatty-looking Maritimers would sneeze and then say, "'Scuse me" really loudly and one of the others would laugh and say, "Ain't no s'cuse fer you, yah dumb mahran!" Pinched faces bearing repressed glares would look up and sort right through a stack of papers. I watched these two masses of humanity interact and I saw myself in the damned film crew, passing judgement with steely looks of condescension. I wanted so badly to play cards with the capers, to sit amongst them with splayed legs, to laugh and joke and play the fool. I wanted to taunt and poke fun at the the film crew, for their rigidity, for their conviction that their lives were better, more ordered, more civilized or some damned thing.

Mayumi, who was beside me, hidden under a covering of blankets, just murmured, neither interested in what I was saying nor irritated for that matter. After all, what did any of this really matter to her? When had she ever expected to have the luxury of travelling in an airplane, when had she ever expected to leave a life of indentured servitude? When had she ever expected to leave a life of being forced to fuck a thirteen-year-old boy, a fat aging salarimen, a portly German tourist, in constant earshot of mama-san?

Chapter 54

Halifax International Airport. The place had changed since I had last seen it, fifteen or sixteen years earlier. Renovations had transformed the airport from a giant rectangular mobile home to a monstrous, ill-shaped government building with wings. As we made our way out to the baggage terminal, though, I noticed the same old dreary rent-a-car booths and tourism billboards with pictures of the *Bluenose* in full sail and Peggy's Cove, waves crashing against a craggy shoreline beneath the heading: "So much to Sea." As we collected our bags, a red-headed man in a tartan kilt blew into his bagpipes and marched up and down on the spot while the rest of the Maritimers on the plane ran into the arms of their loved ones.

A few opportunistic chauffeurs doffed their hats and smiled expectantly. The film people huddled in uninspired little groups with their laptops and cellular phones, yanking up black bags and metal camera cases off the baggage trolley. I noticed, taking Mayumi's hand and walking towards the airport shuttle bus, the usual scattering of pinball machines and video games that no one was playing.

"No friend for drive?" Mayumi asked me.

"No friend for drive, Mayumi," I replied.

"No mother no father? Friend not come."

"No friends, Mayumi."

"No friend? No friend like Toshi, no friend like priest. Long time not see? Wakatta. Wakatta."

And I became angry. I took her arm. "It's different down here for me. I don't really have any friends, Mayumi. That's the thing. I mean when I was young, I never really mixed with people, didn't really make that many friends. Those friends I made I never really stayed in contact with."

"Even now no like?"

"I did have a friend once, a friend that I'm sure I never would have left in a million years if I hadn't been forced into a damned business arrangement with him. His name was Clark. He was a cowboy but he thought he was something else

I suppose. A rock star. Do you know what that is? Rock star?"

"Cock star," she laughed.

"He wasn't at all like that," I began. "He was the purest most honest son of a bitch I ever met. If you met him you'd fall in love with him. All women do, as well as men. I think I loved the son of a bitch. But we were pushed too hard, opposites hurtling through the mess together, holding hands, scared to let go. And when we did, when all the stimulus stopped... Well, eventually you've got to plant yourself somewhere. We're like trees really, Mayumi. Him a maple tree. Hard and strong and sweet. Me a fir tree. All sticky and messy like sap. Bitter. Mayumi. Just bitter."

Mayumi smiled vaguely. "Have house, place to stay?" she asked.

"Yes, well that's the good part. The house where we are going to stay has four bedrooms and two bathrooms and all the space in the world for us."

"Always cold tris place?" Mayumi was shivering, little bluish bumps on her arms.

"Well," I found myself defending this place, "we have seasons here. Summer is like a Japanese fall, and the rest of the time you'll find the whole place very cold. But it really is beautiful, Mayumi. Like Hokkaido, very much like Hokkaido."

Mayumi clapped her hands together. "Kawaii. Suki des." The sound of her voice weakened me.

"Yes, well that's the whole damned thing. The place is damned beautiful. But unless you're born down there, everybody is considered an outsider."

This of course was the wrong thing to say to Mayumi.

"Bakayaru?" she asked. There was fear in her eyes.

"Oh no no." Now I was in for it, deep trouble now. "No, what I mean is you won't be persecuted. It's much more thinly veiled. It's sort of like Toshihiro, when he likes you, he likes you but he doesn't love you. He's more curious about you but he always mistrusts you."

"No like Toshihiro." Mayumi's voice was grave. "Always try sexy sexy. Hairu smeru and aru messy."

"What??" I laughed out loud. The thought of Toshihiro, dark-haired, nervous, breathing hard, ass ripe, pants half-down, eyes blazing. It was funny. There was no other word for it. I said it again, lost the words on the end of my tongue, stared at Mayumi and gasped.

"Do me a favour will you, if you try and speak this language to any of the townsfolk express yourself just like that. Hair smell and all messy..." I clapped my hands together and laughed, laughed for the first time in so damned long. "Hair smell and all messy!"

Well. I shuddered. Well. It didn't surprise me that Toshihiro had tried or succeeded in what he had been after. Any vituperative acts related to that Buddhist priest wouldn't have surprised me, he'd probably had a go at Mayumi as well, and she'd have accepted it as normal, which given the circumstances was normal. Who was I to judge, anyway? I'd shared or turned away or half finished acts with dozens of nameless women with Mr. Sunglasses and Jesse during the years of that tour. Still, something about this possibility did hurt. Hurt and stung and bored into the realm of the unspoken. Something about Toshihiro, about him lingering in my life, bothered me in the same way that Mr. Sunglasses had always bothered me. Something about him lurking and feeding on someone's vulnerability, something about him corrupting the intimate bond that I had established with my own fragile, beautiful woman, something about that... I stopped myself, let the anger abate. I had to let it go. Other things. I had other things to resolve that weren't violent, didn't involve stones in fields or any more fractured friendships. I was coming home and I had to resolve issues that were more immediate.

"We're getting out of here, the two of us." I grabbed Mayumi by the shoulder and she clack clack clacked through the sliding doors behind me. We stood in the freezing fog on a designated wheelchair spot on the main drag, with our bags and Mayumi's little wrapped parcels, waiting for a Zinck Lines bus to shuttle us into Halifax. While we waited, Mayumi's gaze was fixed on a huge, cavernous red building outside, with holes where there should be windows, with plastic fluttering here and there, and at the base trucks and bulldozers all creeping away like shy animals. A great ball was tearing into the side of the thing, demolishing it, and there were workers there, watching it all as well.

"Airu port hotrel," said Mayumi, holding her tummy, trying to read the sign on the side of the building.

"Was the airport hotel," I responded. Everything about it just sagged and yawned. The sides caved in and groaned; boards and asbestos and pink fibreglass, bales of it, lined the side of the road. It all looked so vacant and hollow and I really couldn't see why Mayumi would want to watch such a thing. But then Mayumi turned at me and beamed, with a kind of awe, a reverence and respect that I couldn't and wouldn't imagine.

"Changue," she said, "new building, new building more clean, more comfortable."

Since I had a dickens of a time finding change Mayumi paid the fare. We made our way into Halifax. Then we cabbed it to the Halifax bus station, where we boarded that same grey-and-white Acadia Lines bus that I had taken years earlier, and we both finally made our way down home.

Chapter 55

I found the rector's wife sitting in the back of the nursing home, with a view overlooking the garden. Delphiniums, geraniums, lilies, marigolds, bunches of pinkish flowering chives, pansies and currant bushes. She was in the main window in the sunlight looking down at it all, when I approached her from the back. Twelve years had taken their toll. Her jawline had dropped, and her mouth when she spoke was a reddish purple, as if the veins in her skin were starving off her heart. She was nearly blind too, her eyes watery and downturned, but she smiled when she saw me, blinking myopically, and extended her hands.

"Selwyn it's been so long, so frightfully long," she said simply, and I hugged her as I never had before. I could feel her hand on my shoulder and she patted me as she held me. I couldn't tell if she was shaking or comforting me. All I knew was that I could smell her perfume and her old age and the stale smell of the nursing home. This was an oddly comforting smell, like a pantry or a kitchen with baking bread, and I never wanted to leave.

"There's someone with you, isn't there, Selwyn? Who have you brought, dear? Have you brought a friend along then?" She tapped the floor with her cane.

Mayumi came forward with her head down and extended her hand. The rector's wife took her hand and held it and squeezed it and then finally said, "What dainty little hands, Selwyn, I had no idea you would bring home a Chinese..."

"Japanese," I said, pulling Mayumi back and away. "She's not Chinese she's Japanese and I've married her and she's pregnant with my child."

"Selwyn don't scold me. I'm far too old for this sort of thing. Far too old to be able to tell the difference between a Chinese and a Malay or whatnot. I've always said you've needed a good woman. I'll bet she's a pretty little thing. Does she speak English dear?"

"Better than you speak Japanese."

"Don't be cheeky Selwyn." Her voice was a growl and her eyes were wise and alive and twinkling and I could tell that my remark had delighted her.

In the hallway I heard a murmur and I saw a cluster of staffers smiling in a hands-clasped, patronizing fashion. I shut the door on the blue-jacketed sycophantic lot of them. I knelt down and put my head in the old bird's lap while Mayumi held my hand.

"I feel embarrassed for my behaviour, Gwendolyn, I feel embarrassed that I never wrote you a letter or communicated with you, just shrank away and hid most of the time like a child. It is so damned hard to tell you this; it all seems so ungainly and sentimental and uncivilized to go on about it now but I want to tell you that I really could hug and kiss you, Gwendolyn. I really could hug and kiss you. I can't believe that you're on death's door."

I could smell her old age, and it seemed so beautiful to me, soft and delicate and so fleeting that I luxuriated in what seemed to me a fantasy, the possibility of our both being old.

"Dear dear dear," said Bee, "you are an unhappy soul aren't you? Really I've never understood what all the fuss was about, but there it is, a young man like you who is handsome like nobody's business and so damned sharp in the prime of his life. Well really dear..." And then she coughed, brought her hand up to her mouth and coughed again into an embroidered hanky. Her chest rattled and her face went red and lines grew in her neck. Her teeth inched forwards and I could smell the sour sweet smell of death on her.

"Is it cancer, Bee?" I suddenly surged with fear.

"I'm not sure what it is dear, but the doctor says that I have at least a year and when they say that they're usually conservative with the estimate. So, barring any sudden palaver, I'd say I have at least a year."

"I feel like such a damned bloodsucker, Gwendolyn. Always out for me me me."

"Selwyn, I'm much too old to be your guidance counsellor now. Do just," she said, taking my hand. I felt its stiffness and resolve. "Do just put up or shut up would you dear?"

"But I just want to be happy."

"Well that's what we all want, isn't it, dear?" Then she paused. "You did know that Charlene was back in town, didn't you dear?"

"Charlene??"

"Yes, she and her mother moved back from the States about a month ago." The old woman smoothed over a wrinkle in her afghan as if she were trying to conceal something there.

"Well, is Hector with her?" I asked gulping. "Hector my son?"

"He's at a special school here dear..."

"Well, has Charlene remarried, has he got a stepfather?"

"Apparently the child has been brought up in Scottsdale by his uncle. But Charlene is getting married, Selwyn, and since this won't be easy I might as well tell you now. She's engaged to be married...to Jerry O'Reardon."

Chapter 56

Jesus. Bollocks. Bastard. Dick. I'd put it out of my head, but here it was again. Jerry O' Goddamned Reardon marrying poor Charlene, taking care of my son, whispering terrible, brutish secrets in the poor kid's ears, praising him in public, secretly pinching and poking him black and blue in private, and terrorizing the poor guy while Charlene just accepted this as her life's fate. Jerry O'Reardon who couldn't add two sums with four digits, telling my son, my bright, terribly shy and awkward son, all about life, his life, a life that Hector couldn't comprehend. A life of grenades and plastic bullets and tear gas and AK-47s, nail bombs and dead horses and knee capping, tea and Guinness and Georgie Best. The fact that I hadn't given my own son much thought in the time that had passed didn't seem to concern me just then. It seemed the most natural thing in the world for me to pick up the phone and call her up twenty years after we'd last seen one another and speak to her as if not a single day had passed.

"Where is Charlene living? Do you know, Gwendolyn?"

"She's with her mother till the wedding Selwyn."

"And what day is that glorious occasion?"

"A fortnight Sunday, dear."

Everything else was such a damned swirling uncertain mess that I was determined to let the rest of the business out of the bag. But then I looked at the old dear suddenly and was consumed by a terrible remorse. I took Mayumi's hand and I squeezed it. I froze right there and didn't say a word to Bee about my past. She looked at me with a look that frightened me, a yearning happy look. For me the first time I saw love in her eyes.

Chapter 57

So many things to bring to an end and no time or patience to do it. The pain that I felt was so great that it became a comfort. Knowing that pain was a constant thing, that it wasn't going to abandon me in the way that I abandoned the responsibilities of my life. Mayumi was there with me at the guest house and she spent the first few hours in the bath. She seemed resigned to the place, happy with the simple touristic beauty of the little university town. She said little, just held her tummy and stood for hours in her kimono, towelling off her arms and surrounded by all the wrapped gifts that she had brought for the rector's wife. We made love all that day and into the night and next morning and I fell into her, feeble and despondent, sank in my gloom into her, lost myself in her embrace, in her belly and her loins. I was kissing her as if I would never kiss again; as if I would never feel again. I lost myself in her—let my gloom sink deep into her bones.

Chapter 58

In the morning I felt better. Mayumi was passed out and I wandered down to the lobby in my underwear, holding a glass of water, looking for the pay phone. The woman at the desk stared at me as if I were a tourist, which I suppose I was, even though by rights I was a bona fide citizen of this town. I hated the way she stared at me. "Selwyn Davis?" The woman asked.

"That's right, Selwyn Davis," I replied.

"Well, oh my jumpins. Aren't you the orphan kid that used to go out with Charlene?"

"Some time ago," I replied.

"You got mixed up with that band that was big a few years back, ills and pills er something. And then you hurt a feller and got put in jail."

"I hurt no one but myself," I said, "but I have done some burning in my time."

"I always remember how you used to screech when you was a young feller, all riled up in high school."

For a second it occurred to me that this woman could be a fan. I had spent such a long time away from the limelight that the idea of someone being impressed with some peculiar detail of my own wrecked life flattered me and made me swell with pride and grandeur.

"I was only the singer for a short while, about a year and a half. I never wrote any of the lyrics and I just sang in the band, because they were looking for someone to fill in. Anyone could have done it."

"I remember now, you was travellin' overseas. I read it in the *Sentinel* a while back, then I didn't hear nothin'. Heard the band had an accident and that you'd got yerself fired."

"I never got fired. There was an accident."

"That's right I remember now. But the ills never broke up. They're all countrified now. They're all steel guitars and banjos now. They're still called the ills, mind. But the lead singer is different now. Some kinda cutie I tell you."

"Jaw like a lantern?"

"That's him. Clark er sumpin'." The girl leaned in close. She went all dreamy. "Jeez..." Then she changed tempo. "I hear your mother's dying."

"We're all dying," I said, enraged that she would speak of Bee that way, "and that includes you, you nosy parker."

This offended the girl at the desk and her head went back as if I had slapped her face.

"You haven't changed a bit Selwyn Davis yer still as miserable as you were when you were back in high school. I don't know what the hell Charlene ever seen in yah."

"Because, you whoring little shrew, I know how to make your honey drip."

Her hands were in her face, her face white. "We don't talk rude like that down here, Selwyn Davis. So you've got no right to talk that filthy talk with me."

My frustration was encapsulated in that idiotic moment. Her expression condemned me as a useless human being, and I was unable to tell her in words how ridiculous and rude she made me feel, how ridiculous the whole predicament was, how I was worried about my dear old adopted mother and protective of her. The words had failed me again. My anger collided with my anxiety; a simple miscommunication had rendered her an enemy to me.

Chapter 59

Before I got to dealing with the hell of this whole psychological mess I hoped that I would have some time to myself. I wanted to savour an hour alone with Gwendolyn, drive through the grass-green valleys and up into the mountains, stand by the fields of cow corn and wheat underneath the red silos, stare over at the marshes with the pheasants hiding there. I wanted to see the great dyke lands and drive out past the apple orchards and end up on the red clay soil of the Minas Basin. I wanted to watch the tides rush in, see the basin flood with a deep blue-green and feel the murky red water come towards me, lap up over my feet and shins. I wanted to feel grit in my toes, smell the spoiled dirty-fish stink of dead clams and razor-fish and barnacles, of periwinkles and skate and squid caught under the pier as the sloppy, foamy brine came in. I wanted to pull reeds from the banks, cast driftwood back from where it came, walk along the banks past chewed-up tennis balls and bleached plastic Downy bottles and pretend that I could deal with Gwendolyn. I knew that she would die and that I had no gripe with her and we were still old friends, though her years would now be short and that would be the most terrible and painful part of it for me. Now it was all so anticlimatic. Was there nothing for me here? Nothing for Mayumi? What was it that would make me feel complete?

Chapter 60

I pushed my meeting with the Lockhart family to the back of my mind, away from the impending death of the rector's wife, away from Charlene's imminent marriage to Jerry O'Reardon, away from the pain and suffering of returning to this place with a Japanese wife about to give birth. The subject of my heritage was the most distant thought in my head. I had never seen most of the people to whom I was related by blood, and so I had no petty biases, no irritating biographical tidbits that I could turn into any fantastical case for dislike. I was used to things ending in ruin. I would not shrink into fits of sullen or cowering behaviour when I found they were nothing like I thought. I was not frightened of meeting them, I had resigned myself to it, and in an absurd way expected that this meeting would be the least painful of all. I suppose I dismissed the Lockharts as irresponsible for what they had done to me as a child, but I seemed able to forgive them. I was responsible for my life, the blame was not theirs. I didn't know what exactly I would say, but I was passionately curious to meet, face to face, the woman who had given me up. I wanted to have the courage to stare in the face of my own mother. Marlene.

CHAPTER 61

The man I met in the coffee shop in Wooval was short and bald, with a mustache that looked like he had worn it all his life. His clothes looked like they would fit him and no one else. But I could see in his eyes something of myself, perhaps it was his colouring, or maybe I recognized something in the way he held himself. He was reserved and polite and I could tell the moment I looked at him, as he held the coffee cup in his hand and stared down into the brew, that he was happy to see me. He talked little, apart from saying that he had waited too long for this day. He told me I might recognize his voice, because he had sent that tape to Japan and his name was Earl Stapleton. Then Earl paid for the coffee and we walked silently to his car. I was alone with him, but not uncomfortable. In the scheme of things this was not an unpleasant thing at all.

When I arrived at the Stapleton family farm I was in good spirits, though nervous that they might have Hector waiting in that house for me. I wanted to tell the lot of them that I appreciated their interest in me, but I would point out that they had abandoned me years ago, that I had grown up on my own, and that I intended to keep my life the way it was. I was wary of becoming too friendly with these people, too sentimental. I needed things to play out this way because I felt a simple ending to all this would be the best way for my new life to begin. So with the stench of a strange house thick in my nose, a television that didn't work flickering in my eyes and a series of empty chairs sitting before me, I sat with about twenty strangers, holding my composure as best I could, my head pointed to the floor. At 8:30 the clock struck and a terrible silence came over the house.

"She's not here," I heard a woman whisper in the dark.

"Givver time," one of the men said. "You know how she gets when she's fussin'."

Just then a blaze of yellow and white light appeared in the window, moving across the dirty wallpaper like a great searchlight. The room fell silent, and all faces turned towards the entranceway. In the doorway I saw a familiar face, an expectant and fearful face, a face that bore the colouring of advanced middle age. Grey hair and bright skin and a weight that dragged the pinky jowls down. But there was an excitement in that look, a youthfulness in her eyes that got me. They were the wild, dark-brown eyes that had watched me when I was a surly teenager, that had looked over me with what I was never certain was love or contempt or fear. I saw in this face the eyes of an independent spirit, the sad and loving eyes of my true mother, Marlene.

Not much was said for the first minute or two. The two of us just looked at each other, skeptical and silent like neighbourhood cats, wary of what must be the next move. But then Earl said in his comforting, ameliorating way, "You folks must know each other pretty darned good I'd say. The least you two can do is introduce yourselves. Now Selwyn, this here is yer mother, Marlene."

Everyone in the room, so glum and expectant earlier, rose suddenly in one collective expression of relief. Somebody turned on the lights. All at once there were thirty or more people sitting in a cramped room. And there were balloons there, red and pink and blue like it was my birthday. And don't get me wrong, I appreciated the balloons, I really appreciated the balloons. But it was the sign on the wall that really shook me to the core: "Graydon Lockhart: Welcome home!!!!!"

As the night wore on and my discomfort and shock mutated into a numbing confusion, everything blurred together till I could hear no more. I only knew that I was meant to be Graydon Lockhart, not Selwyn Davis, and that I had been watched with affection by the coterie of aunts and uncles and cousins in this room. They told me I had brought much joy to their hearts, till the terrible day when they found out that I had gotten Charlene pregnant. Besides the bewildering facts of my abandonment and the ridiculous and hurried confrontations between nephew and aunt, nephew and uncle, second cousin and first cousin, first cousin and second cousin twice-removed, aunt this, uncle that, I was struck with the feeling that they were such a terribly common blue-collar lot. My old feelings of superiority had come back. I hadn't changed, I hadn't been able to just shut them out, make them peripheral. They were wandering into that sacrosanct territory that was me. As I became more and more taciturn and withdrawn, my relatives began a hesitant chorus of loving—eyes and hands extended towards me. As I stood there awkwardly, one of them offered to cash in their RRSP for me and the floodgates opened. In a five-minute burst I was offered all manner of support for the rest of my breathing days: babysitters for my new baby, a lifetime of driveway clearing, a freezer full of frozen vegetables, carrots, beans, peas, a box of pickled beets and canned goods, jams, conserves, a fresh-cut Christmas tree every year and a patchwork quilt. Homey things to help me feel like I fit in: a painted house sign, wall hangings, bird feeders, a trio of painted butterflies to tack to the side of the house, little detailed ornaments.

I kept my composure for some time, blinking and listening and watching them till my eyes felt like little glass marbles hardening in my head. I was overwhelmed by their generosity and good favour, but also by my outrage and by the ludicrousness of what this all meant.

"Why was I not told about this in high school?" I demanded.

"Well, we never thought it would develop into something serious, Graydon." Marlene smoothed my hair over.

"Don't call me Graydon, my name is Selwyn."

Marlene looked at me. "Selwyn, please understand. The two of you. We never thought it would get serious. Two fifteen-year-old kids as rare as you two were. We just thought of it as puppy love. We never thought you two would end up havin' sex for cryin' out loud. Have the kindness in your heart to understand. We were in a tight spot there with you, 'cause of what we done in the first place. It was either tell you and risk causing a big fuss by lettin' the whole damned town in on it or hope for the best and pray that yer little fling ding with Charlene'd pass. Honest to goodness we never thought the son of a preacher man would be so interested in getting his girlfriend pregnant. Hell, we were all told Gwendolyn Davies had you all growed up to become a little bookworm anyways."

"Bookworm?? I was hardly that. I was drunk through most of high school as you well know."

"Well that ain't the way you come across there my dear son. You come across as a funny-lookin' little boy who had a weird way 'bout him is all. A little boy who looked like he was friends with his own sister and no more. Sometimes it happens down here a girl grows up and finds out her sister is actually her mother and her Gram is actually her mother. Things can't be told till later on. Selwyn, we just never knew I guess, never knew what it was that was going on."

"That's no damned excuse. Thinking it's alright to leave two confused teenagers together like you did, and expect that because we were so fragile, we weren't capable of even a modicum of human lust. You can't blame a normal hungry adolescent libido on Hugh or Gwendolyn. It wasn't them who failed. They did a fine job with me, a fine job. But you, you should all be ashamed of yourselves... sitting in this room like a crowd of fools. You call yourselves Lockharts. You should call yourselves the yellow hearts is more like it."

"My son wouldn't never of talked so rude."

"Your son..." I scoffed. "If you'd had the courage to keep me and show me some love and kindness, I might have done some good in the world."

"You've been in my heart since the day you left me in that hospital bed, Selwyn."

"I'm thirty-seven years old. I have my own life, my own child on the way. And I've done it without your help."

"We had to tell you, Selwyn. We had to put an end to this sometime, otherwise it just keeps spirallin' and spirallin' and spirallin' like a snowball. Otherwise you're just gonna go on the same."

"And what about Hector, what the hell has happened to him?"

"You don't know?"

"No I don't."

Marlene looked fragile to me just then and I pitied her, standing there as if she was the den mother of this pack of wolves. In that moment I decided I would forgive her, but she would have to endure my feelings, the very miserable complicated feelings I would have in the months ahead.

"Hector? I know he's about twenty or so. And I know that he'll probably be at this wedding."

"You don't know that your son was born with downs syndrome?"

"He's retarded?"

"Mentally challenged."

I stood up. This was all too much. I would not let them see me collapse now. While I had expected the worst, I had not expected this as the capper. I had expected my child to be in school getting a good education, living a humble and honest life. I knew that I still had it in me to forgive. This was my family after all. But not yet. There would be much to endure. I took my mother's hands in my own. "You're a stupid woman, Marlene," I said to her, "obviously a stupid stupid woman. I don't want to hear from you or any of these people for a very long time. You were never there for me and so now I can honestly tell you that I have no interest in being there for you. Don't call me or write to me or speak to me when you see me in town, any of you. Not until I decide—if I decide—that I want to talk to you."

I got up, closed the door behind me and was a solemn face in the car driving home.

Chapter 62

What a nightmare. Home again home again home again. It seemed unbelievable that I was related to those people, and that I had made it out of that house without being laid out on a stretcher. But there was something about them that rang true. Something about the reservation in their eyes. Something in the terrible self-loathing that brewed in and amongst them all. I could see their sloth, their reluctance to talk about anything too serious or important, to make jokes of things. Something of that terrible inertia, that cowardice, that utter lack of interest or awareness in what was really going on, reinforced for me the fact that I was like them.

Yet there was more in me that came from Bee and that was the part that I liked: a sharp wit, a desire for solitude, a passion for foraging through the garden outside, dirt and mud and clay soil caking under the fingernails. For wearing knitted socks with holes in them. For speaking to the cats as if they were old friends. For sitting amongst the flowers in the garden with a frumpy white hat and an old ugly jacket, a wry smile, a cognition. I knew in my heart that she had been there for me as my mother and that right now I just wanted to cling to the old girl who had been my mother.

CHAPTER 63

The rectory was tidier than I remembered it and it had a look about it like it was up for sale. There was a fresh-baked smell and someone had cleaned the place up: the curtains, the stained corners of the house where the compost used to sit. The cracks and stains in the ceiling had been cleaned and painted over. I brought Mayumi into the house and she stared at it like she already had plans. The phone was ringing. Against my better judgment, Mayumi-chan, I answered it.

"'Lo."

"Jeez, Selwyn, you don't sound any different than you did when we were kids."

"Charlene?"

Mayumi glared at me and then sat down in the kitchen on a box. There was a lengthy pause.

"I just talked with Mum and she said that meeting they all planned with you didn't go too good."

"No it damn well didn't."

"I guess you knew about Hector then."

"Hector. You. Mum. Yes, and the rest of it."

"It was just a mistake Selwyn, they were just stuck between a rock and a hard place not saying nothin'."

"That's no excuse, Charlene. We should sue the lot of them you know."

"I ain't suing my own mother, Selwyn, you numskull."

"Look. Save the sentimental attachment for that moron you're about to marry, Jerry O'Reardon."

"Jerry and I are in love, Selwyn, and he is good, real good with Hector."

"They both have the same IQ, that's probably why."

"That's mean, Selwyn, yer own son."

"So's incest. Very mean."

"I'm invitin' you to the wedding you know."

"How pleasant. With my luck it'll coincide with Gwendolyn's funeral."

"She's not dead yet Selwyn. The old dear'll drag on longer than you know."

"Yes." For a moment I felt close with Charlene again. I could just imagine her pushing her glasses up her nose and holding Hector's hand while she spoke to me. "So how come you never called me Charlene, why was it you never wrote?"

"Wrote? Hell, Selwyn, I heard you got chased outta town on account that you burned down our house. Can't blame no one now. What's done is done, Selwyn Davis."

CHAPTER 64

Mayumi hung a Nova Scotia flag and the coloured fish streamers she had brought from Okayama on the old flagpole outside the rectory. She tilled the land outside, organized the lettuce, turnip and horseradish in efficient little rows, planted sakura in the back garden and fashioned a rock garden out of Gwendolyn's old rockery, which she stocked with minnows and goldfish and catfish in lieu of carp. She also began making long pilgrimages down to the flat Minas dyke land wearing a muddy pair of Gwendolyn's rubber boots, an old scarf and an old woollen coat. She started to take a dog with her, a yappy little spaniel that had lost its tail as a puppy (a tractor had run over it). As much as I loathed dogs, I tolerated the little monster, though it had the habit of pissing all over you when you picked it up or tried to pat it.

Mayumi became friendly with the local church ladies, who took her down to the local Baptist church, where she soon became a minor celebrity. She would observe the habits of devout Christians with fascination: grape juice at Communion, story time for children, the modern hymns to go along with their modern and bright church. She was asked to join the choir. Standing there amongst the chubby blue-gowned choir members, she was a dwarf, a little dark-haired Japanese dwarf, knock-kneed in the middle of the lot of them. I felt like she was my contact with the outside world. I did not tell Mayumi of my struggles with my family, for I doubt she would have understood; to her my conflict was ridiculous. For her, a reunion was cause to rejoice. To my wonderment and quiet appreciation, Mayumi developed an affection for those I had long since spurned. I sat and listened while she told me of Mrs. So-and-So's little daughter accepted into a doctoral program at Harvard, a lawyer's wife who was battling breast cancer, a son-in-law who had decided to become a Cub leader, a niece who had won a great prize at 4H, a group of women who had decided to canvass for the Red Cross. These were the stories of the people I no longer understood or had any connection with, because of my own cowardice and anger. And so it was with Mayumi—now darling of the local Baptists—that I finally went to Charlene's wedding.

The service was short and sparsely peopled. I stood there while they exchanged vows dressed up in what I was sure were the best clothes that they owned. Jerry O'Reardon looked like a '70s-era English footballer: long sideburns, hairy arms and a grin like an Irish gnome. He was going bald of course, and still had that glint in his eye, that "I'll laugh at you and you'd better laugh with me" glint. Charlene stood beside him wearing contacts now instead of glasses, a full-figured girl with dimples in her legs. She looked like Little Bo Peep I suppose. A content, plump Little Bo Peep who has found solace in watching soaps on television, sucking stale Diet Pepsi through a straw and downing forkful after forkful of Stapleton's applesauce.

The boy was not there of course, no sign of my twenty-year-old son, no sign of the progeny I had spawned, but never seen. Yet I was notangry at this. What could I expect from this family of yellow hearts? After all, the joke was on them. There I was, sitting amongst them—an embarrassment, a symbol of their guilt and shame. Mayumi let my side me when we came out of the church, spent her time with the crowds of Baptists tittering and whispering and gossiping in little groups. Marlene and the rest of the Family Yellow Heart watched me with the sad and disappointed expressions of people who have lost a child to a religious sect. Not just any child, mind you, but the child that has dibs on a large chunk of the family fortune. It seemed gloomy to me that I was evaluating my life already: I was with a woman who loved me dearly, lived in a house that bore no mortgage, had no real need ever to work again; but I was still enviously watching what others had and had no faith or confidence in what belonged to me.

There was no time for pleasantries, or even an exchange

of rude glares, during the wedding; it just marched along briskly. I watched them both fidget and look bored. Charlene rocked back and forth on her ankles and stifled yawn after yawn as the minister took their vows, and Jerry O'Reardon scratched and pulled at an ingrown fingernail, then turned to the side as he picked his nose. There was no shower of confetti afterwards, no bridesmaid to catch the bouquet or the garter. Charlene changed clothes, pulling on a tight pair of blue Calvin Kleins. She sat there on the roof of someone's car with her ass all dimpled and her feet in white leather sandals, playing a bit with the clasp of her blouse. Jerry hung about talking with Jack and Carl Kenny who looked like they were about to sell him some drugs. The sky was white with grey clouds in it. Charlene and Jerry filed into an old ratty Mustang and headed up to the Blomidon View Hotel, which was situated down a freshly paved road, a path that had once been a logging road. In a different time, Charlene and I had driven down that road and made love, my legs sticking out of the window of the car like twigs. Instead of remaining silent as I should have done, I tried to get a word in with Jerry before they left. I wanted to make my peace with him. I don't know why. I must have taken him off guard. He stared at me while I confessed to him that he had always been a hero to me. I told him I understood the rage that he had felt as a child, and that some of that rage had manifested itself ten years earlier, when I had been wrongly imprisoned for bringing a field stone down on the back of a man's head.

"Don't be stewpid, Selwyn," he laughed with boozy and soured breath. "Everybody knows you're too much of a coward and a cunt to be doing anything like that. Yah haven't changed a smidge, other than we're kids no more. I'll have none of that maimen nonesense. You'll always be a coward Selwyn. You'll always be the one who stands alone. Yah haven't got the courage to fight nobody, 'cause you haven't got a clue what to believe in. Life's pretty simple, once you get down to it, Selwyn. You yah dumb cunt for all your brains don't seem to understand what is plain as day. You act like you're born of privilege, but you come from common stock like the rest." He looked at me one more time. "Just remember this yah dumb cunt. I got on with my life when I left Northern Ireland, don't you think it high time that yew got on with yours?"

These words of truth came from a man who couldn't add, couldn't spell properly, didn't like people much and had just two obvious talents in his life, putting his fingers inside the panties of women I had loved and kicking the soccer ball against the barn door with such velocity that the California earthquake people put his name on a chart. But Jerry was right—no one did care. No one for the most part even remembered me from Adam now. Yes I was the orphaned boy, the stupid sullen fool who lived in his head for years and expected others to solve his plight. Sure my extended family remembered me, and had reached out to me, but it was guilt that made them call my number on the phone, not a sense of really liking me, of wanting to actually get to know the calm and sedate and charming being that I could be. People had moved on, gotten on with their own lives. They had as much interest in my crazy life as I had in what I considered to be their dreary everyday existence: none.

I need to star expressing interest in what I did have: Mayumi, a twenty-year-old son I had never seen and of course Gwendolyn; I had to make my peace with her, now that she was dying, dying as reservedly and as confidently as she had lived. I kissed Charlene after I knew that she was forever gone from me and before she got in the car I asked to see Hector, knowing that I had no choice now but to put an end to this charade. When I got home to the rectory I made a list of the things that were important to me and what it was that I needed to do.

People that matter to me:
1. Clark/Mayumi
2. Gwendolyn
No
1.Gwendolyn/Mayumi/Hector
(Hector has to be slotted here 'cause I've never actual-

ly seen him yet.)

2. Clark

3. Marlene must be in there, she's my mother...

4. I have to change.

Chapter 65

I went to visit Gwendolyn soon after I made the list. She was smiling, sitting near the window in the hallway outside her room with a shawl over her legs. I mistook her facial expression as a sign that she was happy to see me. The truth of the matter was that she was going blind; the doctor had confirmed it that afternoon.

"Selwyn, do be a dear and pass me a glass of water would you?"

"Yes, mother," I replied, sliding the glass along.

"How was the wedding, dear? Did Charlene look nice?"

"Fat and lost," I replied, expecting a quick censure in response.

"The poor dear, she has put weight on hasn't she?"

"It doesn't suit her," I replied.

"How about that good-for-nothing Irishman, Jerry?" Gwendolyn was sipping from her glass. "I never did care much for him."

"Still the same, still the same," I replied. I was growing agitated again. I felt like I had a great weight on my shoulders that I wished to release.

"The doctor was in, Selwyn." I took Gwendolyn's hand and steadied it as she put the glass of water down. "He says I'm going blind, dear. He says what he thought was a cataract is a tumour growing in my head. Seems a bit silly don't you think? Don't you think the whole thing is a bit silly? Him not knowing. You do know who Dr. Stuart Jamison is, don't you dear? The two of you used to go to preschool together."

"Stuart Jamison?" I remembered him vaguely. "I've blocked out most of my past, Gwendolyn."

"It was so long ago. You were such a dear boy, such a dear little boy."

I wanted to talk so badly then that I thought I was going to burst. I wanted so badly to ask Gwendolyn if she could have known that Charlene was my sister and that Hector was my son, that Marlene was my true mother, but something inside me told me I could not. I was not going to ruin the life of an old woman who cared for me and whom I loved as much as I did. Instead, I promised to bring her flowers every week, and then I turned back towards the door. I left her chattering there all by herself. "You wouldn't have thought, would you dear? How would he know? How would he know what it's like to be old and brittle and blind as a bat as well?"

I had one last bit of business that day and I stopped by the drugstore on the way home to take care of it. I bought a postcard for twenty-five cents, a postcard with row upon row of apple orchards and a vista of Cape Blomidon in the background. I took a pen from the dash of the car and drew a cot with a baby in it in the middle of the orchard. The baby was crying. I addressed it to Clark in care of the record company the ills had signed with.

Clark:
You've got to kill the pain
You've got to know its name
You've got to void the shame
and all
and all
and all
that matters

Clark: I always felt like an impostor. But now I've come home.

Chapter 66

Gwendolyn lasted another year and two months in that nursing home before she was taken into hospital. It was another six months in a private ward in the hospital, hooked up to tubes and wires, before she finally passed. After she died, hundreds came to the funeral to express their respect for a woman who was a bit of an oddity and who had always lived on her terms. Some even had the nerve to try to comfort me, but I just glared at them and remained silent.

Bee bequeathed a large sum of money to me, all tied up in old British commodities and textiles that she had inherited in the form of bonds from her father. I cashed them straight away for fear that I might lose them. I gave the money to Mayumi, who shrewdly arranged to have the old rectory sold back to us for a song. At the funeral everyone pilloried me for my coolness and detachment, but the truth is I do mourn the old bird with a kind of sadness that few could ever know. I've spent more hours than I can count in the attic of that house, staring at the old cue cards that she used to turn in front of me when I was a child. On the back are written little notes: Such a sweet little darling, such a clever, clever little boy. Such a little dear. Such promise. Such promise. Reading these now, the pain seeps into my very core and I weep like a scared little child.

Mayumi gave birth to Kenji, our son, and has now set to remodelling our house. And for all of her fascination with the Baptists and the wonders of community suppers and strawberry suppers and all things maddeningly Christian, she has deftly arranged to buy and then sell off blocks of the old apple orchard out the back, which will soon be built into a subdivision. Needless to say, two years after moving here Mayumi-chan has made me a rich man. I suppose I love Mayumi in a way that is as false and as true as life is. I know that I will never be able to give myself to anybody wholly, and that what will bond us together is the love that we feel for our son. And though Kenji is a spirited and happy child, with great promise and cleverness and a sense of joy in living that I never possessed, my heart will always lie with Hector. When I finally did see him, and faced the truth of his origins, and my own recklessness, it all came instantly clear. His poor wretched song at church is the cruellest psalm that I have ever heard.

Chapter 67
Lent

Lent. Two years have passed since I went to Earl Stapleton's house and met Marlene. I sit here now in an empty church pew in the old church, with Mayumi and a quiet little boy who has his mother's disposition and his father's sharp profile. We sit at the back of the church, near the baptismal font, near the old commemorative plaques and the coat rack full of bomber jackets and coats and knitted shawls and hats. Mayumi comes with me regularly now, week after week, as does Kenji, whose bone-white pallor and obsessive fidgeting have made him a likeable peculiarity to the other children in his Sunday-school class. We sit apart from the other families, grouped together as they are in self-important cliques, singing the solemn hymns that we all find in musty old blue-and- red hymn books in the dank wooden shelving.

Other families of twos and threes: the Macintosh family here, the Tillotsons over there, the church warden, whose wife has a stoop about her and appears about to break into a sob at any time, the ancient George Spy, hairpiece and all, rattling when he coughs, the surly church treasurer, who wears the same ill-fitting grey-green Eaton's suit that he wore when I was a small boy, and old Ms. Greer, all tissues and lace gloves, who remembers Gwendolyn as a young woman, before she married Hugh. The other families sit in front of us near Charlene and Jerry O'Reardon. Between them, a smallish young man with jet black hair, fine features and a downcast mouth looks up in awe at the minister about to give his sermon. In my self-imposed exile I am reminded, as the minister begins his Easter sermon, slowly and patiently calming the Sunday school children gathered in the front, extending his arms to entreat the congregation, of God's great grace. The minister speaks with great temerity and resolve about the trials of Jesus Christ, of the Last Supper, of how, in the gospel of St. Luke, Christ healed lepers and ten blind men and only one of the scoundrels came back to thank him. I am reminded, as the minister talks about a crown of thorns on the Calvary cross, about the inscription above Christ's head, about the sabre that is thrust into his chest, of the death and resurrection of our Lord and Saviour. The minister's cheeks turn white and a vein rises in his neck. He begins to yell at the congregation sitting in front of him: And where were the nine? Where were the nine? Where were the nine? At that moment the dark-haired man sitting between Jerry O'Reardon and Charlene, my son Hector, begins to moan and moan and moan so that the place is consumed by the sound of him alone, the sound of his poor wretched moan. It makes me think that he is merely expressing the simple mortal truth that we don't know, we cannot ever know, where it is that we come from.